Single Shot

"For I know the thoughts that I think toward you, saith the LORD, thoughts of peace, and not of evil, to give you an expected end." – *Jeremiah 29:11*

Coffee Cup
Press

Single Shot

Laura Wagenschutz
and
W. Mark Dendy

Coffee Cup
Press

DISCLAIMER

This is a work of fiction. All of the characters, places, organizations, and events portrayed in this novel are either products of the authors' imaginations or are used fictitiously. Any similarity of the characters to persons living or dead (unless explicitly noted) is merely coincidental.

Published by

COFFEE CUP PRESS
244 Fifth Avenue, Suite W260
New York, NY 10001

PUBLISHER'S NOTE

Editor: Maura Reithmeyer

Cover photo (female): Copyright 2011 Phan Tran Photography www.phantranphotos.com

Cover photos (males):: photostock / FreeDigitalPhotos.net

Female Model: Erin Zgraggen

DEDICATION

To God Almighty through which all things are made possible!.

ACKNOWLEDGMENTS

My parents, Mark and Dawn Wagenschutz, for always believing in me. And Benjamin Jossund, my high school principal, who pushed me to write and inspired my love for learning.

Laura Wagenschutz

My wife Zeta for her encouragement, feedback, and knowledge of the scriptures. And the ladies in my life, my wife, daughter, mother, and two sisters for both my understanding and lack of understanding of what women want.

W. Mark Dendy

Both the authors would like to acknowledge David Parr for bringing a young talented writer and an old gentleman holding his own together through mutual friendship!

PROLOGUE

Most people view coffee as their life blood, their one guilty pleasure, self-reward, or soother but we don't typically personify coffee, that is think of coffee as a psychiatrist or anger management counselor. However, there are the few who view their coffee as the one constant in their lives. These are the people on whom the coffee industry thrives. Coffee is the common factor in all aspects of these people's lives. Friends and lovers may come and go, but there's always a Starbucks on every corner – all is well and right in the world. I must admit, that I am numbered amongst this elite group of people.

My name is Nelia Chambers. I live in Jackson, California, a tiny town on the West Coast of these great United States of America. I haven't always lived on the West Coast. I actually grew up in another tiny town, but in the very Northern part of Wisconsin – also known as the frozen tundra. Coffee, like casseroles in that part of the world, is a part of everyone's lives because it is a hearty, hot drink, which is necessary to warm your soul in the frigid temperatures.

My parents thought I was crazy moving to the land of fruits and nuts, but I have to say that I really do love it here. No, my family and friends are not here but Northern California is beautiful and warm. I love the soaring temperatures and the vast array of lakes and beaches to choose from all within just a couple of hours driving distance. Although lonely, California is definitely where I know I am supposed to be. I would, however, like to get a petition to God going to see if we can just fold the U.S. in thirds maybe so Wisconsin and California can be right next to each other. I don't think that would go over very well.

Wow. I am not sufficiently caffeinated for this day.

I am beginning to realize how dependent I have become on my coffee. I never realized how big a role it plays in my life until I moved away from everyone and everything I have always known and loved. Out here, far away from home, family, friends, and familiarity, coffee has become my everything. It's my best friend when I need to talk things out, my sister when I need fashion advice, my boyfriend when I need a hug or a shoulder to cry on, my dad when I need financial advice, and my mom when I am trying to throw dinner together - minus the recipe!

Many of my evenings are spent with Frank Sinatra, my coffee and I cuddled on the couch for a nice, long think. I am not a crazy person – I don't go so far as to talk out loud to my over-sized smiley faced coffee mug (well, maybe sometimes) but he is a great listener to my innermost thoughts and has given me some of the most amazing pep talks! He got me through three years of business school in Boston and I almost had a coronary when I thought I had lost him in the move from Boston to Jackson. Yeah. Losing him would be like losing my head; life as I know it would cease to exist if I lost my coffee cup.

What am I doing in California? You mean, like, besides missing my family like crazy and talking to my coffee mug? Well, I moved West thinking it would open more doors to build upon my life-long dream of having my own vintage book store housed in a quaint Victorian cottage. I would call it "Penny a Page" because, when I was little, I did not like to read at all and my dad thought it necessary to teach me to appreciate reading; he much preferred me reading to sitting in front of the television so he decided to pay me a penny a page for every book I read. I was only five or six at the time so a penny a page seemed like a small fortune. I began reading little books that had maybe fifteen or twenty pages each and my dad paid me accordingly at the completion of each book. Soon, I began to get a bit wiser and started choosing books that had fifty or sixty pages each and so on. By the time he decided to cease paying me to read, the wage per book had gone to a flat rate of one dollar. My dad accomplished his goal of teaching me to appreciate a good book and somewhere along the way instilled a love of literature and a vivid imagination deep within me. This was the seed planted that eventually sprouted into my dream business. My love for coffee came all on its own but fits nicely into my plans as I shall most certainly have a nice little coffee bar in my book haven.

CHAPTER 1

A little over a year ago, I moved out here and spent all of my savings on my apartment and all the logistics of laying the groundwork for "Penny a Page"; I ran out of money before I could actually buy the cottage. For now, I work as the receptionist at a local travel agency and spend every spare moment researching vacant Victorian cottages in quaint little foothill towns like Jackson.

Why does everything have to cost money? Can we not go back to simpler times and trade chickens and such for property? Everyone was happier then and the economy was not in danger because who doesn't have a chicken? Okay. I don't personally have any chickens; but if chickens were our currency I would definitely raise me some chickens! Anyway, until I find what my heart is seeking, I am alone and lonely. Well, not really alone; I do have a roommate, Tamara, but she's never around so I am alone for all practical purposes.

Tamara is the epitome of the social butterfly. Donel, Tam's boyfriend is a consultant for an up-and-coming law firm, so they are always out at different social events and charity fundraisers trying to attract the public's attention. Attracting attention has never been, and will never be, a problem for Donel or Tam. Both of them are graceful giants with excellent bone and muscle structure.

Donel has a darker olive complexion with jet black hair and piercing black eyes, towering above everyone at 6'5", while Tam stands at 5'11" with flowing blonde hair which hangs nearly to her waist, emerald green eyes, and the complexion of a porcelain doll. I, on the other hand, am of the short and stocky persuasion.

At 5'2" I am the exact opposite of my Amazonian roommate. I have drab, dark brown hair that barely grazes my shoulders and eyes that are more brown than green. My complexion constantly makes me look like I just biked 60 miles it's so red (thank God for make-up) and, let's just say, I could stand to lose a few of the 'holiday' pounds from last Christmas.

I'm not jealous of Tam per se, but I wouldn't mind getting even one of the appreciative stares she gets all the time from men. I seem to attract the twenty-eight year old, still live at home, play video games all day and eat Twinkies kind of guys. You know the type. The "so much cooler online" type of guys. Yep. It's my lot in life to attract the dweebs and rejects. I am resigned to a long and lonely existence on this earth and am really hoping God rewards me with a bigger mansion and prettier wings than all my friends who got married right out of college and all had at least one kid by twenty-three. Is that really too much to ask? I think not.

On evenings like tonight when Tam and Donel are out 'on the town' with their equally gorgeous friends, I can usually be found just as I am now – curled up on the couch with my coffee and watching the classic, *An Affair to Remember*. I love my life, don't get me wrong, but, sometimes, it would be nice to feel the camaraderie and sense of belonging that having close friends surrounding you brings. I know my mother would say, "Those aren't close friends, Nelia (she always uses my 'proper' name), they're merely acquaintances – time fillers. They don't really care anything about each other." But, regardless of what my mother would say, I know how I feel and I don't like how I feel.

But what's to be done about it? I don't know anyone here except Tamara and Donel and my bosses, Jim and Sandi. And I'm not the greatest at making friends. Putting myself in situations where I will feel vulnerable is not high on my list of favorite things to do. I could go to Starbucks and sip coffee while pretending to read *Little Women* but actually be scoping the crowd for possible companionship, but that would be ridiculous. Who does that? Really, Nel? Get a life.

I could go shopping but I really don't like shopping all that much. I know. Strange, right? I'm a girl and I do not like to shop. I just don't see the point in spending all that money on clothes that no one who cares will ever see! I work at a travel agency with four people who are all well into their fifties and the only people who ever come into the office are well into their fifties and nobody ever cares what I look like!

I go to Starbucks on the way to work and, of course, the Baristas always flirt because that is what they are paid to do; I could go in wearing a Snuggie and they would still flirt with me. Yes, it makes me feel good momentarily, but then I leave and remember that it's their job - I realize they don't actually give a flip about me as an individual and then my whole day is stinky again.

Okay, you really need to stop getting me all sidetracked. I was going somewhere with this narrative. Oh yeah! So. Remember how I normally spend my evenings? All curled up on the couch with coffee and *An Affair to Remember* or reruns of *Law and Order*? Okay. I was sitting, doing just that, watching *An Affair to Remember* for the bazillionth time on Tuesday night of last week. As I sat stewing about my loneliness, I had an epiphany. It doesn't happen often, but every once in a while I still have a good idea. Honestly, though, it wasn't me; it was God. I was having my pity party when I heard a little voice say, *"Let's be friends."* At first, I thought I was going crazy so I just tried to focus more on Cary Grant; who doesn't want to focus on Cary Grant, am I right? It was at my favorite part of the movie where Nickie Ferrante is asking Terry McKay, "Tell me. Did you write the song 'I'll Never Smile Again'?" I don't know why I love that part, but I do. Anyway. It was just at that part and I could not focus at all. It was almost as if God plugged my ears and said, *NO! Listen to Me! I want to be friends. I can make you happy and give you the companionship and sense of belonging you desire.*

What? I know the verse in the Bible that says He's a friend who sticks closer than a brother and I understand that He is always with me, no matter what, but to be friends with God just seems strange. Right? I mean, I should be out looking for friends my age who are interested in the same things I am and who love coffee – God does not exactly fit that description. I mean – He's God! I decided it was my overactive imagination fueled by insane amounts of lonely that was conjuring up this wacky idea, plus, I had had way too much coffee!

Once again I attempted to focus on the movie, but God would not have it. At that precise moment, all power to my building went out. I fumbled my way into the kitchen and dug through the drawers hoping to find the candles and matches we had stashed somewhere in there. I could not find anything to shed light in my little apartment. No more distractions. God started talking again.

"What is a friend? Is it just someone you hang out with every once in a while to ward off the boredom? Someone you have a coffee date with once a week to catch up on life? Is a friend the person you call when you are out of sugar or eggs? What is so special about a friend? I mean a real friend. They know you, right? They know your ins and outs, your weaknesses and strengths, your tender spots and what makes you tick. A real friend knows you as well as, or better than, you know yourself. Who fits that description better than I?"

I couldn't respond. I was frozen and felt a deep weight pressing on my chest that I instantly recognized as conviction. I knew that I had been neglecting my daily quiet time with Him and my church attendance was kind of iffy, but really? This seemed way too drastic a step even for God. If I were to make Him my Friend, I'd probably never get married and I'd become one of those crazy people you hear about that hides themselves away in a monastery or convent and no one ever hears from again. I want to get married! I want to have kids and go on family vacations and experience all the joys of living my life and leaving my mark on the world!

"Really? You think that being My friend means you don't get to do all of that stuff?"

I don't know. Doesn't it? I thought.

"No. Not at all. I'm your God. I know you. I know the desires of your heart and I know all that I have planned for you. The life you have planned is good, but it's not the best. Are you really going to choose good over mind-blowingly amazing?"

I looked up and whispered, "Well. Since you put it that way..."

The power suddenly came back on and I sat at my kitchen table thinking about what had just happened. Had I really just made a commitment to God, or was it just sort of a casual recognition that He was right but with no commitment attached? I decided to do something I had not done in quite a while and went into my bedroom; reaching into the top of my closet I pulled out my Bible. I had had this Bible since I was twelve and it was highlighted and marked up from the years when I had immersed myself in studying the Scriptures. It had been a while.

I sunk into the plush carpet of my bedroom floor and let the Bible fall open in my lap. It opened to Psalm 73; I began to read. 21 *Thus my heart was grieved, and I was pricked in my reins. 22 So foolish was I, and ignorant: I was as a beast before thee. 23 Nevertheless I am continually with thee: thou hast holden me by my right hand. 24 Thou shalt guide me with thy counsel, and afterward receive me to glory. 25 Whom have I in heaven but thee? and there is none upon earth that I desire beside thee. 26 My flesh and my heart faileth: but God is the strength of my heart, and my portion for ever. 27 For, lo, they that are far from thee shall perish: thou hast destroyed all them that go a whoring from thee. 28 But it is good for me to draw near to God: I have put my trust in the Lord GOD, that I may declare all thy works.*

"…it is good for me to draw near to God:…" I sat in silence, not realizing that I had begun to weep. Realization of what I was rapidly becoming began to seep into my soul. I had been running from the very One who could satisfy my deepest desires and fill every void in my life. The one truly fulfilling relationship I could ever have was the very relationship I had been shunning and even avoiding since I had left my parents' home six years ago. God had been patiently waiting for me to come to my senses and I am just stubborn enough to grit my teeth and push through all the signs and prodding He'd been giving me.

No more. I decided then and there that I would make God my Best Friend. I don't need a guy or a group of friends to complete me or make me feel fulfilled; all that I need is a healthy, thriving relationship with my God. What more could a girl need? God understands the things in my heart that I cannot put into words and He actually listens when I feel the need to talk. He loves me more than anything else and will never dump me for a size two mini skirt. He's my Protector, my Guide, my Confidante, my shoulder to cry on, and my Confidence. What guy could ever be all of that?

CHAPTER 2

I'll have a triple tall, no whip soy milk, caramel macchiato… oh no wait! Make that a quad grande, extra hot, non fat, white… no, forget that."

"Tam," I said under my breath through clenched teeth. "Make up your mind, people are waiting, the line behind us is getting long!"

I could feel may face flushing red, partly due to embarrassment and partly due to my lack of patience – another area of my life that obviously needed some work.

"Tell you what. Make that an iced mocha, quad, light on the ice and add a little peppermint."

"What size?" the girl behind the counter barked. She too was losing her patience, and although slight in stature, her tattoos and the placement of her numerous facial piercings sent a message that she could be one to reckon with.

"Oh yea, make that a venti… no, no, a grande, and give my sweet little friend Nel whatever she wants too." Tam waved her perfectly manicured hand laden with a diamond ring that was worth more than I paid for my last three cars as if to say *go on now, get to work.*

I was trying to avoid any semblance that I knew Tam, but, of course, as always, that was impossible *whenever* I was in the presence of Tam. I knew her actions were well intended, but her flamboyant behavior was so annoying and she always referred to me as her *sweet little friend.* That bugged me!

I ordered a chai tea. I had read that drinking tea was a good way to lose weight. I stepped aside to wait for the barista to get our drinks.

As I stood there, frustrated and humiliated, Tam said, "Look Nel. I think that Barista has the hots for you!" My first instinct was to ignore her comment, but curiosity got the best of me.

I glanced over at the guy preparing our beverages. His forehead glistened with sweat. He was tall, over six feet, and wore tan shorts and a navy blue t-shirt with a graphic design of the chemical structure of caffeine. I could tell he was ripped because the t-shirt fit him like a second skin.

His arms were bronzed and covered with fine blonde hairs. I noticed that his body was free of tattoos, at least the visible parts - his arms and legs and most importantly his head which was covered with hair, perhaps too much! His locks were golden, apparently bleached from hours in the sun, and tied back in a ponytail

He glanced over at me and winked, and I realized I was staring and simultaneously zoning out. I felt my face flush again and I looked down and saw that my arms were covered with red blotches. I felt nauseous, and I turned and headed out the door. I could hear Tam calling, "Nel... Nel, you forgot your tea."

I sat in the car and laid my head on the steering wheel. *Dear God*, I began to pray. *What is wrong with me?*

It had been less than two weeks since I had had that "You don't need a guy – I'm your best friend" discussion with God, and here I was looking at a guy and thinking, wondering, *could we be a couple?*

The sad part of it all is he wasn't even my type! I could never picture myself with a "surfer" type with or without the tattoos. A guy that probably smokes marijuana, rides around on a motorcycle when he's not surfing, and changes girlfriends more frequently than he changes his underwear. That's what this guy was; I just knew it! His vocabulary probably consisted of mostly four letter words, and if someone mentioned Jesus to him, he would probably say something like, "Nah, I never met the dude, but I'll betcha he's really cool with a name like Jesus."

What am I doing? There's something seriously wrong with me Lord!

I banged my palms on the steering wheel, and I began to sob.

I heard a knock, knock, knock.

"What Lord? What do you want?" I shouted. My eyes were shut tightly, tears seeped out, and my forehead was now pressed against the steering wheel.

"Open the dang door Nel before I drop your tea!"

Tam wasn't smiling as I flipped the passenger door handle and pushed the door open.

"What is wrong with you today Nel? Are your hormones out of whack? Can't you tell that Lance is interested in you? Or are you oblivious to the fact that he was ogling you?"

"What? Who?"

"Lance, the Barista. He has an eye for you!"

"No way! You have been out in the sun too long today Tam. You're delirious!"

"I swear Nel. The guy likes you! Did you see him wink at you today? And every time we come here when he's working, he always steals glances at you. I'm telling you Nel. Lance is sweet on you!"

"Well you are dead wrong Tam. I am not that guy's, Lance or whatever his name is, type… period!"

"Well whose type are you? Mr. polo shirt, debate team captain, bury myself in a research lab and only resurface for church three times a week type?"

"Very funny. I know I am not his type and he is *definitely* not my type."

"How do you know?"

"I just know! End of discussion!"

We got in my car and rode to our apartment without another word.

I went straight to my room and shut the door.

Sitting on the edge of my bed, I could not get the recurring negative thoughts out of my mind – *What is my problem? There is something seriously wrong with me!*

I reached for the Bible on my nightstand, but it slipped from my fingertips and fell to the floor open. I stared at God's Word lying there on the floor and it seemed to call to me.

Kneeling in front of the open book, I saw a single verse underlined in blue ink and highlighted in pink.

"Before I formed you in the belly I knew you; and before you came forth out of the womb I sanctified you…"

As I looked up, a ray of sun pierced the leaves of the tree outside my window. The sunlight warmed my face and my tears began to dry.

"I know I belong to you Lord," I shouted, "but what should I do about Lance?"

I was feeling guilty for having *any* thoughts about Lance. I knew nothing about him; yet based on his physical appearance, I, of all people, had passed judgment on him.

I began to wonder. *Should I go up to him the next time I see him and introduce myself. Try to find out something about him? What are you telling me God?*

I went out to the living room to talk to Tamara. She was sitting on the couch in a yoga pose. Her eyes were closed and I felt jealousy deep in my bones.

Why can't I be like her?

A scripture entered my mind before my thoughts could continue.

"I will praise Thee, for I am fearfully and wonderfully made; marvelous are Thy works, and that my soul knoweth right well."

I remembered my mom reading to me from the book of *Psalms* when I was in middle school and I would come home from school crying because the other kids were constantly teasing me; I found strength in that scripture then, and I found strength in that scripture now.

I whispered, "Tam?" Her almond shaped eyes opened wide. She had a soft smile on her lips.

"Can I talk to you?"

"Sure. What's up?"

"Do you think Donel is the man God has chosen for you?"

"Well yes… why do you ask?"

"How do you know? What makes him different from all the others?"

"I don't know. He's just… different!" she shrugged.

"Well that's definitive." I mumbled.

"What's going on with you? You've been acting a little strange lately, and this morning… I thought I might have to call the men in white coats to take you away!"

"Tam, you know I don't do well in situations like that! I'm not gorgeous like you and I don't know what to say, and…"

"I know you are not like me. You are nothing like me! But that's okay. Tell you what. Watch me tomorrow when we go in for our morning caffeine fix. Watch how smooth I am with Lance."

"But I'm not you Tam! I don't look like you; I don't act like you, and I don't talk like you."

"So?"

"And besides…"

"Besides what?"

"We're going through the drive-thru from now on!"

CHAPTER 3

In spite of Tam's insistent whining and nagging, I had effectively avoided any encounter with Lance for almost an entire week. I was feeling rather victorious in this particular area and was proud of myself for figuring out that Lance never worked the drive-thru. On this particular morning, however, as I rounded the corner and began my approach to the window I saw him. At first it was just a hand coming through the window with a steamy cup of joy for the lady in the bright blue sports car in front of us, but then I saw a nicely bronzed arm attached to that coffee and soon Lance's whole head and chest were sticking out the window as he stretched to reach the lady's hand. .I watched in disbelief as he flashed her a killer smile.

Oh, no. I thought. *Please, Lord, anything but this! Do you hate me, God?*

I was hoping that Tam had not noticed him. She continued babbling about the new line of something or other at Macy's and I tried to calm my jitters, thankful that Tam was oblivious to my distress. The blue sports car slowly pulled away and I saw a bejeweled hand toss a flirty wave back to Lance. He smiled and waved back.

Oh brother. And Tam thought he was into me? What a laugh!

Just as I rolled my eyes Lance glanced our way and our eyes met. He froze for only a moment and I slowly inched the car forward, or so I thought. Our trance was broken by the honking horn of the car behind me. Lance disappeared back through the window and I released the brake. Tam looked at me like I was losing my mind, but kept talking. *Lord, give me strength.* I prayed.

We came to a stop just below the Drive-Thru window and waited. I stared straight ahead, afraid of what I might find if I looked toward the window. I heard the window open and then there was silence for a few seconds. I tried looking sideways without making it noticeable when Tam slapped my right arm.

"What the heck are you doing, Nel? Pay the girl!"

It was a girl! Praise Jesus! I turned and smiled, so relieved to find a twenty-something blonde Barbie standing there. "I'm so sorry! I haven't had my coffee yet this morning; don't know where my mind is."

She smiled back. "It's cool. You'd be surprised how many people zone out before getting to this window." She swiped my card and handed it back to me. "Your drinks will be ready in just a sec!" The window slid shut and I sat there grinning.

"You are so weird."

I looked over at Tam. "What?"

She sat sideways in her seat just staring at me. "Why do you keep zoning out, chica? What's going on with you?"

I opened my mouth to answer just as the Drive-Thru window opened. I turned to reach for our coffees but didn't make it before Tam was nearly in my lap and talking, "Hey, Lance!"

Oh you have got to be kidding me. I glanced toward the window and, sure enough, there stood Lance holding my chai.

"Hey, ladies. How are you this awesome Summer day?"

He sounded like *Crush* from *Finding Nemo*.

Tam giggled. "You're so funny, Lance!"

I sat silent.

"Isn't he funny, Nel?" Her elbow dug into my side. "We've missed seeing you, haven't we, Nel?" Again, her elbow dug into my side as she glared at me.

Silence. They both were staring at me. "Um. Yeah, I guess."

"Totally groovy!" His head bobbed up and down. "Well," Lance lowered his head and looked around like he was about to share some government secret with us; his voice became a stage whisper, "I've kinda missed seeing you but don't tell the others." He winked one of those dramatic, face-contorted winks and Tam began giggling uncontrollably.

Oh brother. I reached for the coffees and took them out of Lance's hands as quickly as possible, shoving them at Tam. "Thank you!" I shouted as I hit the gas. I just wanted to be away from the entire situation. Away from Tam, away from flirting, and definitely away from Lance.

We sat in silence as I concentrated on crossing the two lanes of traffic in order to get going the direction I needed. Tam was pouting, I could feel it. My face was flushed with embarrassment and I took off out of the parking lot a bit faster than I maybe should have. Tam's latte almost went flying but she caught it just in time.

"Hey, watch it!" Tam's eyes were wide in disbelief.

I mumbled, "Sorry."

"What's the deal, Nel? There's something else going on here besides the fact that you don't think you're Lance's type. Talk, girl."

Drawing in a deep breath, I decided it was time to tell my roomie about my decision.

"You're gonna think I'm crazy."

"Um. Kinda too late for that warning, don't you think?" She crossed her arms and waited for me to speak.

"Probably true. Okay. So, you've noticed I've been on edge the past couple of weeks....."

The talk with Tam went over a lot better than I thought it would and she even agreed to lay off the matchmaking a bit after I explained my decision to forget guys until I could honestly say God was my best friend. I dropped her off at Donel's office and headed off to work.

I got to work a little late, but no one seemed to notice. The way the travel agency is set up, I can see everyone else's desks from my desk in the lobby, and I noticed as soon as I got in that everyone was acting a bit strange. I scoped out the situation.

Jim, the owner of our little travel agency, was noisily slurping his morning coffee and seemed to be intently studying something on his computer screen. Sandi, Jim's wife, sat in the office to his left filing her nails and seemingly trying to avoid looking my direction. Lee, Sandi's brother, sat in the office directly across from hers and he seemed to be engrossed in a travel magazine, but he appeared to be rather fidgety too. To his left was Jack's office. Jack was shuffling papers nervously and nearly jumped out of his skin when his phone rang, "He… he…hello?" He fumbled with the receiver which he was holding upside down. He righted it, "Hello?" *Something was not right,* I thought.

I stashed my purse in the bottom drawer of my desk and made my way over to straighten the pamphlet rack on the right side of the lobby. I heard the door behind me open and I turned to see the best looking man I had ever laid eyes on standing before me smiling. He stood near six feet tall with broad shoulders noticeable even through his perfectly cut pinstriped suit. His dark hair was neatly cut and fashionably styled and he wore a classy pair of Armani glasses.

"Good morning." His voice sounded the way I'm sure a robust French Roast would sound if it could speak. He held out his hand, "My name is Nic. Nic Spaulding."

I couldn't speak but I somehow managed to shake the man's hand just as Sandi came bustling out of her little office. "Oh! Good! You're here. Finally! Come in, come in. Please come to Jim's office. Would you like some coffee? But of course you would, why am I even asking? I should know you better than that. Go. Go, sit down. Jim, he's here!"

Sandi pushed Nic toward Jim's office and turned to get him coffee from the pot in the corner. "What are you gawking at, girly, get to work! Make yourself look useful!" she shooed me back toward the pamphlet rack and scurried away to get the coffee.

I was so confused. *Who is this guy? I've never seen him before.* Maybe he was a relative of Sandi's? She hurried into the office and briskly shut the door.

I went back to straightening the pamphlets and hadn't even finished when Jim's office door opened again and Nic emerged with a goofy grin on his face; he nodded in my direction, looked me up and down once, chuckled and headed out the door. I checked my outfit. My royal blue blouse was buttoned properly, my khaki pencil skirt wasn't twisted sideways or anything and my shoes were a matching pair. *What was so funny?*

The entire day felt slightly off with everyone in the office acting as though they were keeping some great secret. Just as I was getting ready to lock up for the night, Jim and Sandi called me into Jim's office. I sat in one of the stiff chairs opposite of Jim and waited awkwardly in the silence. Jim cleared his throat loudly and Sandi nudged his shoulder in my direction. He sighed. Sandi became too impatient and spoke up.

"Nel, we've so enjoyed getting to know you in the bit of time you've been working with us. You've become like the daughter Jim and I never had; you're such a dear. You're always asking if there's anything else you can do or baking cookies for people's birthdays and anniversaries. Remember the time you came to the house to help me clean after I had surgery?" I nodded, somewhat befuddled as to where this conversation was going.

"Well," Sandi said, "we know a little about how you were raised and we've sorta noticed you haven't been real happy lately."

Oh brother. Is it that obvious?

Sandi continued. "I know when I'm getting down a bit or just kinda lonely or something that what I need is some good Christian fellowship. You know there's nothing like getting together with a group of fellow believers and…"

"Oh, good grief, woman, get to the point!" Jim huffed. He leaned his arms on his desk and looked at me over his glasses, "You told us you were raised in church but you never talk about going to church here. Have you found a church home here in Jackson, Nel?"

They both looked at me, Jim expectantly and Sandi almost anxiously.

What did they expect me to say? I wasn't about to tell them the commitment I'd made to God or about the inner turmoil I'd been having since then about needing to find a church to join but I did feel I owed them an honest answer.

"Well, no, not really. I've visited a few in the area but none of them really seem to fit me or the way I was raised. But I am looking." I hoped that would appease their sense of duty to making sure I was doing right.

They looked at each other and Sandi smiled. "We would like you to join us for services this Sunday, Nel. And, of course, we'd love to have you to the house for Sunday dinner! Lee and Jack will both be there with their wives too. We all go to church together. Did you know that? It's so nice. We have such a lovely time together and-"

"Sandi!" Jim interrupted. "Let the poor girl speak."

I was unsure how to answer. I didn't want to hurt their feelings, but I didn't want to commit to going to their church either.

What if I don't like it? What religion are they anyway?

I didn't even know. A brief shadow of guilt passed over me momentarily at the realization that I hadn't even thought to talk to my coworkers about God but it quickly passed and was replaced again with the awkward silence staring me in the face in the form of Sandi and Jim's expectant gazes.

"Uh…." *Well that was intelligent, Nel. Great, definitive answer.*

"You don't have to decide right now," Jim told me. "You just come if you wanna. We go to the little Baptist church up on the hill; it's called Straight Paths Baptist. Sunday school's at ten and morning service is at eleven. Okay?"

I nodded, thankful for the opportunity to turn them down by simply not showing up rather than doing it face to face. "Sounds good to me. Thank you for the invitation."

Laura Wagenschutz and W. Mark Dendy

CHAPTER 4

I stopped at Panda Express on the way home and ordered my usual – chow mein with orange chicken and honey walnut shrimp. I debated whether or not to have fried wonton too, but decided against it because I still wanted to shed a few of those extra "holiday" pounds.

What will four little fried wontons filled with cream cheese hurt?

No Nel, remember you're trying to lose weight.

But they can't be more than a couple hundred calories.

Nel, remember, you have to start somewhere!

The debate went the same way every time, only the foods changed!

I drove home thinking - *Friday night at home alone… AGAIN!*

As I opened the apartment door, I sensed something different in the apartment. Usually I would find the apartment bathed in whatever fragrance Tam had decided to don for Donel for their night out. But tonight, the scent in the air was quite different. It was fragrant like Tam's *Vera Wang "Preppy Princess"* but with a tinge of muskiness that burned my nostrils ever so slightly.

There was a note on the coffee table written with purple sharpie. The handwriting was signature Tam!

Have fun with your new mate Nel. Call him whatever you like!

An arrow pointed to my closed bedroom door.

This better be good Tam! I thought.

I took a deep breath, closed my eyes, turned the doorknob, and pushed the door open slightly. I could see my dresser and the corner of my bed. Oh, and the pile of laundry that could keep me occupied on yet another lonely Friday night.

I pushed the door open a little farther.

"Hello? Hello? Is anybody here?"

Silence.

"What kind of game is Tam playing with me?" I said out loud as I plopped down on the bed and dialed Tam's cell phone.

Tam answered on the second ring. "Did you find him?"

"Who?"

"Him!"

"Him who?"

The words lingered on my lips as my mouth fell open. Standing the doorway to my bathroom was the most adorable gray kitten. He had four white socks, a white belly, and a white moustache. Tam had put red lipstick on his little moustache and he had a royal blue collar studded with rhinestones wrapped around his neck.

"You found him huh?"

"No Tam, he found me," I chuckled.

"Call him whatever you want. He doesn't have a name."

"Oh Tam. He is so beautiful and so soft! Mozart. No wait. Figaro… His name is Figaro!"

I curled up on the couch with my Panda Express to watch reruns of *Law and Order*. The difference between this and all other Friday nights was I had Figaro to join me.

Despite the heavy honey walnut glaze on the shrimp, Figaro had a nose for seafood and bounded across the room his little legs propelling him upward onto the couch where he snatched a morsel of shrimp. That made me smile and then I thought of how dad would be lecturing me about how unsanitary it is to allow a feline to get near my food. I remembered getting busted by dad one day when I was five or six feeding my cat, *Buttons*, bits of my tuna fish sandwich under the kitchen table. That made me laugh out loud!

I missed everyone back home. I decided to call Rachel, my sister. It was only 7:30 so with two hours difference I knew Rachel would be up. I might even have a chance to talk to my twin nieces, Summer and Winter. They were in their terrible twos now, and adorable as ever. I had been home for Christmas and loved the way they loved their Auntie Nel! They both had dark hair and blue eyes like their dad and their temperaments matched their names. Summer was always bright and cheerful and Winter could be stormy and cold as ice!

Winter answered the phone. "Helwo. Who dis?"

"It's Auntie Nel."

"MOMMY MOMMY Aunty… WHO'S DIS?"

"It's your Auntie Nel!"

"Nel?" Rachel had grabbed the phone.

"Hi Rachel! How are you?"

"I'm okay. Just dead dog tired! Shopped all day dragging the girls with me. Came home and crashed. When I woke up, Ron had given the girls ice cream and they are all wound up. Winter! Stop hitting your sister!"

"I'm sorry Nel. Is everything okay with you? Can I call you back later? This is just bad timing"

"That's okay Rachel. Call me when you can. Okay? I love you. Tell Ron I said hi and give the girls hugs and kisses!"

"Okay Nel. I'm sorry. Love you. Bye!"

"Bye, Rachel."

"Well Figaro, looks like you and me are alone but together!"

I scrubbed my face and brushed my teeth while Figaro peered at me through the open bathroom door. I crawled into bed but couldn't sleep at all. Figaro, on the other hand went out like a light while I was rubbing his belly. His purring turned into snoring. Cute but annoying after awhile.

Thoughts of Lance and Nic were nagging me. I stared at the ceiling fan as it went round and round. That didn't seem to help. I watched the red LED digits of my alarm clock change one to the next. That didn't seem to help either.

At 12:30, I opened my Bible to Psalms 33 to try and find comfort. *"Let all the earth fear the LORD: let all the inhabitants of the world stand in awe of him."* I skimmed a few verses and then He once again revealed His purpose to me… *"For our heart shall rejoice in him, because we have trusted in his holy name."*

He was speaking to me once again telling me that He understands the things in my heart that I cannot put into words and He actually listens when I feel the need to talk.

I was awakened by the warm sunshine beaming through my window. My Bible was lying open on the bed, and Figaro was curled up by my side still snoring. My pillow was wet with drool. Yes, my drool!

It was Saturday morning, the time when I typically did laundry and cleaned the apartment. As I mentioned earlier, Tam was hardly home, so most of the mess was invariably mine.

Figaro remained at my heels all morning as I scurried around the apartment tidying things up and doing laundry.

When Tam left my little surprise, she supplied all the necessities for having a kitten – food, kitty litter, cat box with a filter system to remove the odor, and a kitty bed in a basket, which, of course, Figaro shunned, choosing to sleep with me instead. I cleaned the cat box and gave Figaro fresh food and water.

My work was done by 11:00 a.m. about the time Tam was getting up. I had a fresh brewed pot of coffee so as our typical Saturday ritual went, we sat on the patio and chatted about our Friday evening and discussed plans for the remainder of the weekend.

As we talked Figaro sat scratching at the screen door and meowing to come out and join in. I told Tam that there was a free outdoor Jazz concert in the neighboring community of Sutter Hill and was thinking of taking Figaro with me.

"Do you want to come with me?"

"No. Donel is taking me to Jackson Rancheria for the afternoon. and besides, you know I hate Jazz Nel! But you go and take Figaro. Maybe you'll hook up with a cute guy! "

"Oh brother! Have you already forgotten I gave up on guys?"

"Oh that's right. Yep, I forgot," she said with a bit of sarcasm.

"So what are your plans for tomorrow?" I asked.

"Donel and I were thinking about going to a different church tomorrow. Pastor Bob is out of town and so there having a missionary from Bosnia speak. Boooorrrring!"

"Where are you thinking of going?"

"Come with us! It's a little church on 6th street up on the hill. I think it's called Straight Paths Baptist."

I was shocked and spewed coffee out.

"Have you been there before?"

"No, no."

"Why were you so shocked? I hear they have a dynamic young pastor who's single," Tam said practically singing the words 'who's single!'

"TAMARA!"

"Okay, okay, but come with us."

"Let me think about it."

Donel arrived to pick up Tam in his black Land Rover just as I gathered up a blanket, sunscreen, and a couple of bottles of water, and stuffed it all into my I ♥ *Wisconsin* bag. Tam opened the door and yelled "Be right there!"

Figaro, seeing an opportunity to go outside and play, darted between Tam's legs and right out the door. He ran around the back of the apartment building and down a short hill into a ravine.

I ran out the door and around back and spotted him lying underneath a patch of blackberries.

"Figaro. Here kitty kitty." I took a couple of steps and he turned and ran about five yards further into the thicket.

"Tam. Grab my flip flops for me."

Feeling guilty for having let Figaro slip out, Tam was in and out of the house in a second. She handed me my flip flops.

I called again. "Here kitty kitty." He inched towards me in a crouched stance. I met him halfway, the weeds and briars scraping my bare legs.

"Don't you run away like that again," I said as I picked him up and clutched him close to my chest.

Holding Figaro tight, I picked up my bag and got into my car for the short trip to Sutter Hill, halfway between Jackson and Sutter Creek. There was not a cloud in the sky when we arrived at the *Italian Society Park*. Temperature was in the mid 70s.

"Let's see how you handle walking on a leash," I said to Figaro as I clipped the matching royal blue leash to his rhinestone studded collar.

"Mew, mew." His little kitten voice cheered me as I opened the door. Figaro bounded out of the car and strutted until he reached the end of the short leash. His tailed waved like a flag.

"Wait a sec little buddy. Let me get my bag."

I found a little patch of unoccupied green grass near the base of an old Oak. I thought momentarily about what it would be like to be sharing that little patch of grass with Lance or perhaps Nic, but those thoughts quickly dissipated as I immersed myself into sounds of Jazz and I played with Figaro.

At nine o'clock Sunday morning, Tam knocked on my bedroom door. I had just gotten out of the shower and was wrapped in a towel.

"Morning Tam," I said as she opened my door. For some reason Tam felt like she could knock, count to three and just open my door. I had become accustomed to that.

"So, Nel. Are you going with Donel and me to church?"

"Oh man, I completely forgot. I was going back to "Country Oaks Missionary Baptist Church.""

"No. No. No you're not. You're coming with me and Donel and we are taking you out to lunch after service."

"But I…"

"No buts! Donel is picking us up at 10:30." She turned and marched out.

"How do I stand up to her?" I asked Figaro.

"Meooow!"

"You're no help!"

Donel arrived to pick up Tam and me at 10:30 on the dot. Donel was always punctual.

As we got in the car Donel said, "Just in time. We can still stop for a mocha."

Oh brother!

Donel ordered for the three of us and as we pulled up to the drive thru window he reminded me, "Be careful not to spill!. This is real leather!"

I slid down in the seat as we pulled up to the window hoping not to see Lance.

Tam leaned over Donel and yelled through the window, "Is Lance working today?"

"No, he never works Sundays. Says it's against his religion," the perky blonde said as she passed the drink carrier to Donel.

Tam turned and winked at me. "Judge not that ye be not judged!"

As we pulled away I felt this burning itching sensation all over my legs. I scratched but that made the itching worse. Red welts began appearing from my ankles to my knees. My face began to itch. I scratched it and rubbed my eyes.

"What's going on back there Nel?" Tam asked. She turned around and by the look on her face I knew things weren't good. "Look Donel!"

Donel stopped the car and turned around. "Holy mackerel Nel… you're all broke out!"

"I don't know what I could be allergic too. Maybe the thought of Lance makes be break out in hives," I halfheartedly said with a chuckle.

"Oh my gosh Nel. I bet it's poison oak!" Tam said.

"But where would I have gotten poison oak? The park?"

"FIGARO!!" we both blurted out simultaneously.

Tam turned to Donel as she said, "We need to get you home!"

CHAPTER 5

What? Home?" I screeched. "Should I not be going to a hospital?!" I could see the red streaks appearing on my arms and legs and my face felt like it was on fire.

"No, silly, you'll be fine. I think we just need to scrub your skin to get the oil off and you'll be fine." Tam said as she slapped Donel's shoulder. "Drive faster, babe!"

We got to the apartment and Tam helped me inside and into the shower; a shower had never felt as good as it did right then. Forty-five minutes later, I was slipping into a tank top and basketball shorts hoping to avoid any unnecessary contact of my skin with anything. I suddenly needed coffee. My chai that Donel had bought earlier was long since cold and I was in the mood for something stronger anyway. I waddled to the door and out into the living room. Donel and Tam had gone online and found that Straight Paths Baptist Church actually live-streamed their services and were watching the end of the Sunday school hour.

"Oh! Come watch with us, Nel!" Tamara patted the cushion beside her. "I think the new pastor is preaching next."

I groaned inwardly. "No thanks. I think I'm gonna try to read for a while." I headed for the kitchen. "Do either of you want coffee? I'm going to make some."

Neither of them wanted any, so I made just enough for one cup and headed back to my bedroom. As I shut my door I could hear the new pastor of Straight Paths welcoming people to the service. His voice sounded vaguely familiar. *It couldn't be.* I stopped for a moment and listened but by that time the music had started playing again and I shook my head to push away the suspicions niggling at the back of my mind. *There's just no way,* I thought. I shuffled over to my bed and grabbed the copy of *The Musician* off my night stand. Figaro was curled up asleep on my pillow so I crawled onto the bed and laid on my belly leaving my legs sticking over the edge. The less contact they had with the world the better.

I woke up around 3 o'clock Sunday afternoon to Figaro licking my face. My body felt like there were a million ants crawling all over me. "TAM!" I bellowed as I pushed Figaro away. The last thing I needed was for him to catch my rash on his poor little tongue. "TAM!"

She came rushing into my room. "What on earth? Why are you screaming at me?"

"Can you just shoot me? Put me out of my misery?" I mumbled partly because I meant it and partly because my face was buried in my silk comforter.

Tam sighed. "No, I will not shoot you. Why don't you take a shower again and try some lotion or something?"

"I don't think that'll help."

"Well," there were a few moments of silence before Tam shared her next best solution to my torment. "You want me to give you a pedi?"

I called in sick to work on Monday and, by lunchtime, I'd received calls from all of my coworkers. Sandi had promised to bring me food for lunch. I graciously accepted. *The less movement I make,* I thought, *the better for me.*

Since it was only Sandi coming I had decided to stay in my tank and shorts instead of trying to find something else to wear that wouldn't make my skin burn even more. By now my legs, arms, and face were bright red and a few painful blisters were beginning to form.

I heard a knock at the door and waited, hoping Sandi would just come in. There was another knock. *Grrrr. I love you, Sandi, please, please, please just come in so I don't have to get up.* A third knock. I crawled off my bed trying not to touch my skin against the comforter and slowly made my way to the door. I swung open my front door and quickly slammed it shut again.

What on earth?! This has to be a nightmare!

I slowly drew closer to the peep hole and squinted to see who was standing at my door. I wasn't dreaming. Nic Spaulding stood on my doorstep holding a To-Go bag from Chile's. What was I supposed to do?

"Hello?" He was speaking to me. My breath caught in my throat. "Hello, Miss Chambers?" he chuckled and waited for a response.

"Uh." *This cannot be happening to me.* "Hi."

He laughed again. "Hi. Sandi asked me to bring some lunch by for you. She said you aren't feeling well?"

"Um. Yeah. Thank you. You can just leave it there!" I was praying he would just put the bag down and walk away. I was sure he didn't see me when I opened the door because he was looking at his phone.

"Well," he glanced around uncertainly. "Well, I would be inclined to do that except for the fact that Miss Sandi practically threatened me with poisoning if

I didn't see you for myself and give her a full report of how you're doing." Nic looked at my door expectantly.

I'm going to strangle the woman in Christian love. "Um. Okay. Uh. Great."

I could see his smile growing as I continued spying on him through my peep hole. "I promise I won't care what you look like. I've seen poison oak before and I know it can be… well…Ugly!"

I hesitated for a brief moment more and then cracked my door open just enough to stick my head around the corner. "I'm fine. Thank you. And thank you for lunch." I reached for the bag and Nic stared at my flame red streaked arm. I quickly pulled it back inside. "I promise, I'm fine."

"Are you sure? That looks pretty painful. Do you need anything?" He looked genuinely concerned.

"You might want to try some calamine lotion. It will relieve the pain. Would you like me to go get you some?"

"No, I'm fine. Really." I reached again for the bag. "Thank you though."

"Ok. If you say so." He had that goofy, lop-sided grin on his face that I'd seen when he was leaving Jim's office. I didn't want to ask what it was about but I did want whatever food he had brought. He handed me the bag. "Have a fabulous day, Miss Chambers. Perhaps we'll meet again soon." He walked away leaving me speechless.

I watched him walk to a black Chevy Volt and climb in. He glanced over his shoulder in my direction as he reached to shut his door and I quickly slammed my own hoping he hadn't seen me staring at him. The food smelled good. My stomach rumbled and I realized I hadn't eaten anything since yesterday afternoon. No matter how glad I was to receive the food, Sandi was going to be in trouble the next time I saw her.

Tam came home Tuesday evening with a Walgreens bag and a Cheshire Cat grin. "You'll never guess!" she jumped up and down a couple times, clapping her hands like a freshman cheerleader.

"You've discovered a way to scrape my outer layer of skin off at home without killing me?"

"Nooooo." She drawled. "I stopped for coffee this morning and guess who was working. Well, it was Lance! And…. Are you ready for this? He asked me where you were!" Tam looked at me with a huge grin on her face, "That's good, right? It shows that he really *is* interested in you, Nel!"

I couldn't believe it. *Could this week get any worse?*

"I doubt that he's interested; he probably just noticed that you were alone. We always go together so he's just observant. That's all. What's in the bag?"

Tam rolled her eyes dramatically, "That's what I'm talking about, Nel! He asked me where you were and I told him what happened and-"

"You *told* him, Tam?!"

"Yes. But get this!" she was waving her hands at me to follow her to the couch and she reached into the bag as she began speaking again, "I told him what happened to you and he got all concerned and everything and he said his brother had poison oak once and that I needed to buy this lotion for you. So I went to Walgreens after I left Donel's office and I found it, so now you can't be mad at me for telling him, can you?" She ended her tale with a big cheesy smile and her hands holding out a bottle of Calamine lotion as if she were a model on The Price is Right.

I squinted at her and reached for the bottle. Grabbing it from her hands I said, "*IF* it works you're forgiven. I suppose."

Tam chuckled as I walked to my bedroom and shut the door. "I'll let you rub yourself down! You can buy my coffee in the morning when you're miraculously healed!"

By Thursday afternoon my rash had stopped burning and itching and I was able to return to work with the intent of giving Sandi a good talking-to. But

Sandi wouldn't let me get a word in while she raved about the qualities of their new single pastor. It was a very long day.

Sunday rolled around again and I was determined to not attend Straight Paths Baptist Church even though Tam and Sandi had both been on my case about it since Thursday. I woke up at 2 a.m. and couldn't fall back asleep. I grabbed my Bible and shuffled to the kitchen to make coffee. God wasted no time to start telling me why He woke me up at such an early hour.

"So. You're not going to church today, I hear."

"Well… I wasn't exactly planning on going. But I have this rash and my church clothes will rub it and make it itch and burn and then…"

"Stop making excuses. What did I tell you about church? I said not to forsake the assembling of yourselves together, right?"

I thought for a second. "Maybe."

"There's no maybe about it, Nel. You're going to church today."

"But… I…"

"Stop! You're going."

How does one go about making excuses to God? He kinda knows um, *everything*. There was no wriggling out of this one; I knew I would have to attend church today. I grabbed my cup of coffee and my Bible and padded my way into the living room for some quiet time with Him. I prayed for strength and wisdom and that I would get more sleep before I started the day. I was going to need His strength if I was going to make it through without totally humiliating myself.

I walked into the back of the sanctuary just as the congregation was standing to sing. I noticed the pews were comfortably filled and spirits were high. I found a seat very near the back and slipped in beside an elderly lady wearing a brightly colored dress and a straw hat with a large red flower on the front. She smiled and handed me a song book as everyone began singing.

I stole a glance at the platform and spotted Nic Spaulding standing just behind the song leader's left shoulder. What was he doing here? He was wearing a gray pinstripe suit, a white shirt, and bright green tie with a matching pocket stuffer. He was smiling as he sang and surveyed the crowd. Our eyes met and his smile widened a bit. He nodded in my direction and seemed to be waiting for me to respond. I nodded ever so slightly and I noticed he stood a bit straighter as he moved his gaze to take in more of the parishioners. I was shocked when he stepped to the pulpit and announced the text for that morning's sermon. He's the new pastor?!

My goal was to get through the service and sneak out before anyone spoke to me. I sat through the message which was pretty good, but I was rather distracted by the fact that Nic was the pastor. How could Sandi have failed to mention that? By the time Nic was making the final announcements I decided it was now or never and slipped from my pew to make my way to the lobby. Just as I turned to make my escape I ran smack dab into a very tall, very buff man. I guess I must have made a noise because Nic and everyone else in the church seemed to turn and look at me in unison. I looked up at the man I'd collided with to find myself staring into a familiar face.

"Lance!"

CHAPTER 6

When I came to I was lying on a couch in the Pastor's office. Lance, Nic, Sandi and Jim, and Tamara and Donel were all staring at me.

"What happened?" I said, still in kind of a fog.

"You fainted!" Lance and Nic said in unison.

The only other time I had fainted was in sixth grade when Billy Mercer slipped a frog down the back of my shirt on the school playground.

"You don't look so good," said Sandi. "I think you have been overdoing it sweetie."

"We'll get her home and put her to bed," Tamara said as she and Donel each took an arm and began to lift me up off the couch.

My immediate thought was, *Hallelujah! Saved from any more humiliation.*

"Not so fast," Nic said. "I think she should stay right here, and I will look after her for a while. You know I work in Shingle Springs as a volunteer EMT."

Tam and Donel laid me back down on the couch, and Lance stepped back, palms up. "Whatever you say dude!"

Jim and Sandi being good followers said, "Pastor Nic's right. He's the one that should watch over you. Let's leave the two of them alone. Thank you so much Pastor for taking charge and reminding us of our places!"

Donel took Tam's hand and led her out. Lance stood at the foot of the couch in silence until Jim and Sandi shooed him out like herdsmen herding a goat through a gate.

Lance had a worrisome look as he glanced over his shoulder and mouthed the words *See you soon.*

That Sunday afternoon seemed like an eternity. Several times I tried to get up, but Nic insisted I stay down.

"I am trained in knowing when a person is okay. OKAY!"

I wanted to call Tam to come and save me from this guy. There was a point when I hoped that Lance would ride in on a white horse and rescue me. I was ready to settle for Lance riding in on a Harley and rescuing me

I lay there on the couch and all Nic talked about was Nic! I heard about everything from his high school achievements and awards to his heroic rescues of people trapped in wildfires in the Sierras. He told me about his college romances. He even gave me a synopsis of his Valedictorian speech at Liberty University.

All along I thought – *This guy really needs to read Max Lucado's book "It's Not About Me!"*

I could only imagine what could be worse than that Sunday afternoon – *Sinking in quicksand? Being gored to death by a bunch of wild unicorns?*

Tam and Donel returned to the church a half hour before evening service. They never attended services other than Sunday morning and I was hoping today wasn't the day they decided to change.

"Can you take me home now?" I asked as I sat up on the couch.

"Feeling better?" Donel asked with an ear to ear grin.

"I just want to go home."

I stood up. Nic stepped in front of me and placed his palms on my cheeks. "Let me see those eyes."

I didn't want to make eye contact; I just wanted to go home. In fact I was afraid if I looked into Nic's eyes or heard anymore of Nic's stories, I would throw up! In order to make my escape though, I knew I had to do it. I looked straight into his eyes and forced a half smile.

"Well, looks like you're good to go! I'll see you soon," Nic said. "It was great getting to know more about you."

"Likewise," I said still forcing a half smile.

I headed for the door behind Tam and Donel.

"Let me walk you out to the car."

"No, no. That's okay. You've done enough."

"I insist Nel. I won't let you dismiss me that easily," Nic said taking my hand as if we were a couple.

We reached the car and he opened the back door for me.

As I sat down Nic said to Tam and Donel, "It was a pleasure meeting you. Now take good care of Nelia. She's special!"

SPECIAL? I thought. *Anybody that would listen to a guy babble for hours on end about themselves has to be special!*

As Donel pulled away from the curb, Tam turned around and asked, "How was he? How was your afternoon?"

I made a gesture sticking my finger down my throat and said, "Don't ask!"

CHAPTER 7

J im gave me the week off and I found myself sitting at Starbucks Tuesday afternoon with my laptop open and a caramel macchiato sitting by its side. I was so relieved to see Lance was not working when I entered the coffee shop. I sat with my back to the door and had my ear buds in listening to my Michael Bublé station on Pandora, tuning the rest of the world out. My morning had been spent immersing myself into the world of real estate. I was in way over my head. My gaze was locked on my computer screen and I was kicking myself for not wearing my glasses when I felt the sensation of being watched. I sat up straight and found myself staring straight at Lance who was sitting across the table from me.

"Where'd you come from?" I squeaked.

Lance laughed. "I've been here a while. You were pretty focused on whatever it is you're looking at. Not surprised you didn't notice me." He sipped his drink and glanced around the shop.

I studied him carefully. He was wearing a loose-fitting white t-shirt that made his tan appear deeper than I remembered. His *OP* board shorts seemed out of place in Jackson, California, but they suited him oddly enough. He had on flip flops and a braided leather bracelet encircled his left wrist. His head came back around and he caught me looking at him. I blushed and looked down, flustered not only by being caught but also by the adorable grin that crossed his face just as he found me studying him. He leaned forward slightly and whispered, "I'm not a stalker, I promise. I come here even on the days I don't work." His smile widened and he said in a normal tone, "What's life without God and coffee, right?" He lifted his drink to his lips and took another sip.

"Yeah, I guess." I wasn't sure how to respond to him. He wasn't exactly what I had imagined him to be. He seemed comfortable with who he was but not cocky, confident but not arrogant. Maybe I had been wrong in my assessment?

He tapped his fingers on the table and glanced around a bit more. Taking a deep breath he looked back at me and said, "Sooo...." He drawled. "Nel, right?"

"Yes." *Where is Tam when I actually need her? What on earth am I supposed to say to him?*

"Cool." Lance's head bobbed up and down. "Is it short for anything?"

"Um. Yeah. Nelia."

"Nelia?" My name rolled off his tongue gently and something inside me tingled a bit.

What on earth!

"I like that. What's it mean? Is it a family name?" He was leaning back comfortably in his chair with a sincerely interested look on his face.

"Uh. No, no it's not a... a family name. It's actually Gaelic and means Champion."

"That's so cool!"

I just looked at him, completely at a loss as to what to do or say. I bit my lip. *What would Tam do?* I found myself reaching for my phone to text her.

"So you actually *do* drink coffee, I see." Lance grinned and waited for a response. When none came he chuckled, "I'm not gonna bite you, Nel. I'm a nice guy. I promise."

I grinned and shook my head slightly.

"Ah! There it is!" he said loudly. "I knew you had that pretty smile in there somewhere."

I laughed. "Are you always this……"

"This what? Charming? Awesome? Intriguing?"

"Loud."

Lance threw his head back and laughed a deep belly laugh. I could feel people staring and felt my face flush bright red. *Oh my soul. God, please just make him go away.* "I'm sorry." He chuckled and looked at me. Our eyes met and he stopped, "Has anyone ever told you your eyes sparkle when you're embarrassed, Nelia?"

My jaw dropped. I felt my face flush and I fumbled for something, anything, to say. Nothing came to me.

"I'm sorry." He waved his hand in front of him as if to erase his question. "I didn't mean to embarrass you, I promise. Forgive me?" he flashed me that killer smile but it wasn't teasing this time, it was sincerely asking forgiveness.

"Uh. Sure. Yeah. Yes, of course, you're forgiven." Lance wasn't at all what I thought. He had blown my picture of him out of the water in less than ten minutes. *Wow. Was I really that far off or is he trying to throw me off?* I couldn't decide.

Lance looked like he was about to say something else when I heard a familiar voice behind me call my name. I turned to find Nic making his way to our table. *Oh, this is just perfect. Could my life get any more awkward than it is right now?* I found myself wishing Tam would walk through the doors and come to my rescue but she was in Santa Clarita visiting her mom.

"May I join you two?" Nic was pulling a chair from the next table as he asked. I knew nothing I said would dissuade him, so I said nothing.

"Hey, Pastor Nic." Lance said as he studied my face. I was trying to 'play it cool' as Tam would say, but I felt I was failing miserably.

"Oh, hello." Nic barely acknowledged Lance and leaned in close to me. "How are you? Are you feeling better? Your eyes look bright and alert; I think you'll be fine. You're looking well anyway. I haven't been able to get you off my mind, Nel." He reached for my hand, "Have you missed me?"

I pulled my hand away from his grip and clutched my hands together tightly on my lap. "Uh. Honestly? No, I haven't." Tact had never been one of my strong suits. Lance was trying his best not to laugh, I could tell.

"Oh." Nic sat up straight. "Well. *That* was unexpected." He looked at Lance and Lance met his gaze unwaveringly. "What are you doing here?"

"Just having a cup of coffee with a friend." The two men stared at each other briefly before Lance looked at me, "We were just leaving, right, Nel?" He raised his eyebrows and nodded his head ever so slightly as if to say, *Just trust me. Say yes.*

"Uh. Yeah. Yeah, we were just leaving." I quickly shut my laptop and gathered my purse and phone and reached for my empty coffee cup. Lance's hand beat me to the cup. He nodded as if to say, *Trust me, Nel.* I nodded back and he took the lead.

"Here, Nel, let me take your stuff." Lance tossed our empty cups into the garbage can behind his chair and reached for my laptop. "We'll see you at church, Preacher." With that, Lance put his hand on my upper back and led me to the open door of the coffee shop. I tossed a glance back toward Nic and saw him still sitting at the table looking rather dazed.

As soon as we were out of the shop Lance dropped his hand to his side. "Was that okay? I promise I wasn't trying to make you uncomfortable."

"No! That was good. Thank you so much!" I had apparently been holding my breath because I let out a sigh that seemed to come all the way from my toes. Lance laughed. "That was really awkward!"

"Nah. You were great." He smiled down at me.

Wow. He's really tall. I thought. *Maybe I'm just really short. Hmmm. What am I thinking? Why am I even thinking about this? It doesn't even matter. There's no way he would ever date me.*

"Hey. You okay?" Lance stopped in the middle of the parking lot and looked at me.

"Uh… Yes?"

He looked skeptical. "You were like, totally zoned out or something because I was definitely talking to you and you were definitely not responding."

"Oh. Sorry. I'm fine, really."

"Okay, if you say so." He started towards my car again, "So, what do you say?"

"What do I say about what?"

"You really were ignoring me. I'm hurt, Nel!" He placed his hand over his heart. "Deeply hurt!" he said with a laugh.

"No. Really I wasn't ignoring you. I promise! I just…. didn't hear you."

"Uh huh. Sure." I glanced up just in time to catch him winking at me.

Oh brother. I'm not sure I even want to know what he asked. "What was it you asked?" *Why did you just ask him that, Nel?!*

"I asked if you might be interested in going to Sutter Hill on Saturday night. They're having a folk music concert in the park. I saw you there a couple weeks ago and thought you might like some company this time." He looked nervous and confident all at the same time; it was kind of cute.

"Oh. Well…" I wasn't sure how to respond.

"You *do* kinda *owe* me for saving your life back there, ya know." He flashed me a smile. "The very least you could do is go on one date."

I thought for a moment. *It couldn't hurt anything, right? It's just one date.* "Okay. Yeah. I guess that would be alright."

"Yes!" Lance shouted and threw his fist in the air as if he were a boxer claiming the victory at the end of a match. My brow creased in concern. "Oh." He shoved his hand in his back pocket. "Sorry. Too loud?"

"Maybe just a tad." I chuckled.

"Well. I'm kinda excitable if you haven't noticed." Lance handed me my laptop and I gave him my address. "Great! Pick you up around five then. And don't worry about eating dinner before then, we'll pick something up on the way."

Oh great. Does he really think fast food is a good first date? "Sounds good." *What on earth am I getting myself into?*

Tam was ecstatic when I told her I had agreed to go with Lance to the concert and wanted to know every detail of our conversation. An hour and a half later, I hung up and decided dating was way too much work. I would go on this one date but make it very clear to Lance that I was simply repaying him for getting me away from Nic. That would be the end of it. After Saturday I would not go on another date, even just as friends. Lance wouldn't understand my commitment and desire to know God as my best friend so maybe if I'd just mention that he'd leave me alone? However it ended, I was sure it was going to be a long night.

CHAPTER 8

Friday evening rolled around and I looked forward to Panda Express and reruns of *Law and Order* with Figaro. Hopefully that would take my mind off of my date with Lance.

All week long my thoughts were dominated by the upcoming Saturday outing – what to wear, what to say, how to broach the topic of living for God. Like I said… *dating was way too much work!*

I heard a rumbling noise outside my apartment. I went to the window and peered out. It was Lance on a Harley. Not just any Harley, but a real loud Harley with ape hanger handlebars and a half naked woman painted on the gas tank.

He was wearing a denim vest that looked like he had changed his oil while wearing it. It was opened in the front, and underneath, he was shirtless. His jeans were ripped I'll just say in places where they shouldn't be!

I had no backdoor to escape through. *What should I do? What can I do? How much worse could it get?*

It seemed as though I was about to find out. Nic pulled up in his black Chevy Volt.

Why me Lord?

I looked at Figaro and screamed "HELP!"

Next thing I know Nic rushes into my apartment and grabs me.

"Are you alright?"

I'm being shaken.

I pushed away with all my might. "NO!"

"Wake up! WAKE UP NEL!"

I opened my eyes and Tam was standing over me. She was dressed in pink shorty pajamas. "I think you were having a bad dream."

"No Tam, it was a full blown nightmare!"

I couldn't sleep the rest of the night worried about my "date" the next day. I got up at 5 a.m., fixed a pot of coffee and called Rachel. It was seven o'clock in Wisconsin, but I knew the twins would have her up early. *Besides*, I thought, *this is an emergency!*

I was right, Rachel was up We talked for more than two hours. I always looked to Rachel for advice. She was level headed and smart, and she knew and understood the scriptures.

Rachel was extraordinary in every way. She was absolutely beautiful and graceful, the kind of beauty that graced the covers of magazines. The kind of beauty seen on billboards across America.

When Rachel met Ron and began dating him, she was a junior in high school. I was eleven and in sixth grade. Everyone knew Ron was not Rachel's type, especially me. He was a total geek, wore mismatched clothes and goofy glasses, and stuttered when in uncomfortable situations. His nickname was "Foo," and to this day even Rachel doesn't know where that came from. Despite what everyone else thought, she seemed to think he was the man

God had in mind for her, and daddy loved him! I didn't understand what Rachel saw in Ron, at least not then. But I watched their love grow over the years, and they celebrated their eight wedding anniversary this past Valentine's Day.

"Why didn't you call me sooner?" Rachel asked. "You know I'm always here for you."

"I called last week but…"

Rachel interrupted me in mid-sentence. "Oh Nel! I am so sorry! You did call me the other night, and I put you off. I am sooooo sorry!"

"That's okay, but I really need your advice now!"

I explained everything that had taken place over the past two weeks from Jim and Sandi trying to fix me up with Nic, to not being able to get Lance off of my mind in spite of the fact he was not my type. I ended with last night's nightmare.

"Have you prayed about the situation Nel?"

"Of course I have Rachel! Well sort of… uh, not really!'

"Well sis, get your priorities straight and see if things don't fall right into place."

"You're right."

My sister had a way of getting me back on the right course. She could be gentle but harsh at the same time, if that makes sense.

"Love you Rachel."

"I love you too Nel. Call me after your date with Lance."

I pictured her smiling after she hung up, and imagined her bouncing the twins on her knees and singing, "Auntie Nel's got a date, Auntie Nel's got a date!"

Tam got up later than usual. I had finished one pot of coffee and had just made a second, fresh pot. My chores were done including all my laundry – a first for me.

We sat on the patio and drank coffee. I had put sliced cantaloupe and grapes in a bowl on the table. Figaro, was accustomed to being in and out now. He curled up in a ball on the chair between Tam and me.

"Sooooo, are you ready for your hot date?" Tam inquired as she popped a grape in her mouth.

"It's not really a date Tam. I'm simply going with Lance because I am grateful for him saving me from Nic Spaulding!"

"Whatever!" Tam said flipping her hand in a gesture to add emphasis.

"What do you mean whatever? Why don't you believe me?"

"I see the way your eyes sparkle when Lance is near or when you talk about him!"

"Whatever!" I couldn't help but smile.

It was killing me that I kind of liked the guy, but *what if he was really like the Lance in the dream?* I couldn't fathom that!

"So only a couple more hours. What are you going to wear?"

Gosh, I hadn't even thought about what I was going to wear.

"What do you think I should wear?"

"Oh, that's easy! Cut off jean shorts where your rear hangs out, a halter top, and stiletto heels. And we can go to Walgreens and pick up some neat rub on tattoos for you, maybe a snake and a skull. How about the grim reaper?"

"Stop it Tam," I said smacking her on her arm. "Seriously!"

"I am serious hon. You'll make a hot biker babe," she said with a chuckle.

"How about my white capris?"

"You might get grass stains rolling around on the grass with Lance."

"Come on Tamara!"

"Okay, okay. Either your white capris or the tan ones with the two buttons on the outside of each leg. And you can wear my sleeveless teal blouse."

"Oh thanks Tam. Now what about shoes?"

"Flip flops should be fine, but if you want to look sexy for Lancie boy, you should wear your cute *Daisy Fuentes* wedge sandals."

"Well, I am not aiming for sexy, but those sandals do look good on me."

"Oh, hang on a sec!"

Tam ran into her room and returned in less than a minute with nail polish remover, cotton balls, and Caribbean blue nail polish.

"You are going to have the prettiest, sexiest toes at the concert!"

I went to my room and sat on my bed. Figaro had followed me in and jumped up onto my lap. I closed my eyes and tried to think of how to start my conversation with God. He had always been so easy to talk to. *Why is it so hard now?*

I reached for my bible and opened it to Psalm 121. I began reading.

"I will life up mine eyes unto the hills, from whence cometh my help. My help cometh from the Lord, which made heaven and earth. He will not suffer thy foot to be moved: he that keepeth thee will not slumber. Behold, he that keepeth Israel shall neither slumber no sleep. The Lord is thy keeper: the Lord is thy shade upon thy right hand. The sun shall not smite thee by day, nor the mood by night. The Lord shall preserve thee from all evil: he shall preserve thy soul. The Lord shall preserve thy going out and thy coming in from this time forth, and even for evermore."

Once again He spoke to me, and the words seemed to flow from the depths of my soul.

"Precious Lord, Savior of mine. I am so grateful for your constant presence in my life. Lord, I know that it is through you that I can have the peace that passeth all understanding, and Lord, I know I am yours. I ask that you give me the opportunity to share Your Word with Lance this evening. Give me the strength and the wisdom and the words to demonstrate tonight that even though I live in the flesh, Christ lives in me. In Jesus precious name, Amen."

A calm fell over me until I looked at the clock. It was quarter till five!

Lance will be here any minute and I'm not even dressed. YIKES!

"Tam! Bring me that shirt!" I shouted as I jumped in the shower.

I was in and out of the shower in record time - two and a half minutes

Tam had ironed the shirt and my pants and had them laid out on my bed. She also had small dangling earrings and a matching necklace of hers on my dresser waiting. When I wasn't looking, she dabbed the back of my neck with some of her *Elizabeth Arden "Pretty Hot"* perfume!

I slipped into my wedges and said, "How do I look?"

"Fabulous, my dear, simply fabulous! I'll bet Lance's jaw drops the minute he sees you!"

There was a loud rumbling noise outside the apartment. I looked at Tam and said, "We need a back door in this place."

"Come on," she said as she grabbed my hand and dragged me towards the front door.

Tam looked through the peephole. "You are not going to believe this Nel!"

"Don't tell me it's a motorcycle. Please don't tell me that."

"Oh no. It's not a motorcycle. See for yourself!" Tam swung the door open wide and strutted out to greet him. "Hi Lance! Nice car!"

I could not believe my eyes. Lance was dressed in knee length gray plaid shorts and a black Nike polo shirt. His hair was neatly trimmed and tied back in a pony tail. He had just stepped out of a shiny 1968 fire engine red Chevy Camaro convertible. The top was down and I could see the white vinyl interior was as meticulously cared for as the exterior. I could hear the song *I Can Only Imagine* by *Mercy Me* sounding crisp through the CD player that probably cost as much as my car.

What is this guy's game? I expected him to show up on a Harley? And the music? I had pegged him as a Hip Hop fan or maybe a metal head. I think he's messing with my head.

Everything about this guy and his motives seemed questionable.

"Where does a barista get the kind of money it takes to buy an original muscle car like this? It must be worth 12 or 15 thousand," I pointedly asked Lance as if I was a prosecuting attorney and he was the defendant.

"Actually, it was appraised three years ago at 32 k."

"Really?" I asked as I walked around the back of the car. "Oh this explains it," I said as I eyed the personalized license plate – *DAD'S TOY.*

"Not quite," said Lance not the slightest bit annoyed with my implication. "I'll explain, but first I want you to meet someone."

This is odd. He asks me out on a date to a concert. Shows up in daddy's car, and then wants me to meet someone. Oh well. I just have to make it through this evening.

He turned the car around and headed south out of town.

"I hate to tell you, but Sutter Hill is the other way."

"Bear with me for a few minutes. Remember you owe me!"

We drove about five miles out of town. I was enjoying the sun and the breeze as we rode in silence with the top down.

"I don't even know your last name, Lance."

"Dupont."

"Dupont? As in Dupont chemicals?"

"That's right," he said nonchalantly as he turned onto a gravel road leading up a hill to a beautiful Victorian.

"Where are you taking me?"

"To my house."

"Oh, I get it. You're taking me to meet mommy and daddy for their approval. Isn't it a little early for that?"

"No, I want you to meet my sister."

Wow! This is getting weird!

We walked up the steps to the grandiose porch. Lance opened the door, took my hand, and led me into the entryway which sat at the base of a spiral staircase.

"Amanda! Come here I want you to meet someone."

"Just a minute," a voice came from another room.

I was nervously tapping my foot. I said, "Lance, we're going to be late for the concert."

About that time Amanda came around the corner – in a *wheelchair*. "Hi. You must be Nel!"

"How did you know?"

"Lance hasn't shut up about you since he first saw you."

I felt my face flush.

"And you must be Amanda, Lance's?"

"Sister. I'm Lance's sister."

"I can see the resemblance." *Tan, blonde, that goofy but endearing smile!*

"Amanda spends the summers with me along with Christmas and Spring break. She goes to Stanford."

"That's great. What are you studying?"

"Pre-med. Keeps me plenty busy. And I have all my therapy there."

"Therapy? What happened?"

"Lance! You haven't told her yet?"

"No Amanda. I haven't. I just haven't found the right time."

"There is never a right time," Amanda said scolding Lance.

"Why don't you come in and sit down, and I'll tell you."

"Amanda! I was taking Nel to a concert at Sutter Hill. We'll be late!"

"That's okay Lance. We don't even have to go. I would like to know more about you." I was really curious now.

"Well, I guess." Lance sounded defeated.

I followed Amanda as she wheeled herself into the decadent living area.

"Have a seat," Amanda said holding her hand out towards the plush couch.

I sat down and Lance sat beside me.

"Lance? Would *you* like to tell her about our family or shall I?"

"I'll tell her," he said nervously.

"When I was nine years old I went to Washington, D.C. to stay with grandma and grandpa for the summer. Mom and Dad were on their way to pick me up the week before school started. We lived in Ocean City. They were driving westbound on Highway 50 just east of Cambridge, Maryland. It was just after nine in the morning. A drunk driver pulled out and headed the wrong direction. He hit my dad's car head on instantly killing my mom and dad." Lance's eyes welled up. I took Lance's hand in mine as he continued. "Amanda was in her car seat but the impact snapped her neck leaving her paralyzed from the waist down. She was one year old at the time."

"Oh, I am so sorry. I have said such insensitive things. Oh gosh, I feel so bad!"

"You didn't know Nel! The Camaro I'm driving is the car that my dad drove my mom to their prom in. He had it completely restored so they would have a great memory. Amanda had the idea for the personalized license plate. Mom and dad left us, well me, lots of memories."

Lance was trying to curb his emotions.

"Is it too late to go to the concert Nel?" he queried.

"No," I said gently squeezing Lance's hand.

"Why don't you come with us Amanda?" I asked.

"No. Just the two of you should go. I don't want to be a third wheel. Lance has been waiting all week for this night!"

CHAPTER 9

We drove for some time without speaking. Lance's stereo was apparently on a shuffle mode because it had gone from playing *Mercy Me* to *Kari Jobe* and was now playing *Scott Krippayne's "Sweet Company"*. The picture I had made in my mind of who Lance was seemed to be quickly crumbling to pieces; I wasn't sure if what was being revealed was actually the true Lance or merely what he wanted me to see. I was rather perplexed. Lance reached over and turned the volume down.

"I'm sorry if that kinda threw you for a loop, Nelia." I'd not seen this serious side of his personality before. "I didn't mean to put a damper on anything but Amanda really has been wanting to meet you, so I thought, since you may never speak to me again after tonight, I should probably take you over there while I had the chance."

"What?!" I was confused. *Why wouldn't I speak to him after tonight? What's he got up his sleeve? Maybe I should call Tam and have her and Donel come rescue me.*

Lance glanced over at me and chuckled. I was hoping he couldn't see what I was thinking. "I just meant that seeing how I don't know if you're gonna give me a second date I should probably introduce you two today."

"Why on earth would you say that?"

"Say what?"

"About a second date. We haven't even finished one date, what would make you already be thinking about a second date?" I was hoping I didn't sound too insecure. It had been a while since I had been on a date and I honestly did not see any reason a guy like Lance would want one date with me let alone ask for a second.

"Oh, believe me," Lance said quietly, "I'm thinking long past a second date."

I felt my face flush bright red. I wasn't sure I wanted to know what he meant, but I suddenly felt at peace. It felt right somehow to be in that car next to Lance and on our way to a concert, just the two of us. I felt a smile slowly creeping across my face and looked down at my folded hands in my lap. Lance must have seen it because he asked, "What's that for?"

"What?"

"You know what." He grinned. "What's with the smile?"

"Nothing." I looked the opposite direction, hoping he'd not see the flush of my face or the fact that my smile was ever widening.

"That's not a 'nothing' kinda smile, Nel." He reached over and touched the back of my hand with his fingers. "I'm glad you said yes."

I sat for a moment, staring at his hand resting comfortably between us. I liked the way his fingers felt against my skin, but I was thankful he hadn't taken my hand in his.

That would have put me over the edge. What's going on with you, Nel? Get a grip! This will never work. It's Satan trying to tempt you. I suddenly had a thought. *That's it! This is Satan trying to tempt me away from my commitment to God!* I decided to play it cool the rest of the evening and not be overly friendly or interested in Lance's life. No matter how much he pressed for a second date, I would remain firm and decline. I felt my spirits deflate a bit, but I knew I had to stick to my guns.

Lord, please help me just to say and be what You want me to say and be tonight and just make Lance see it'll never work between us. Show it to both of us, God?

My prayer was interrupted when Lance asked, "You like picnics, right?"

"Um. Yeah?"

"Good. Because I packed us a picnic." He flashed me a smile and I felt my resolve melting just a little. *Picnics are my favorite, God! Really? Why couldn't he have just pulled through McDonald's and offered to buy me a Happy Meal or something? He'd be easy to dislike then.* This was going to be much more difficult than I'd thought.

Lance found a parking spot quickly and insisted I wait for him to open my door for me. He grabbed the picnic basket out of the back and we headed off to find a patch of ground to claim. He chose the exact spot Figaro and I had shared at the previous week's concert.

Was this just ironic? Or divine intervention?

He pulled a blanket out of the basket and spread it on the ground. I sat as close to the edge of the blanket as I could get, putting as much distance between us as possible. Lance glanced at me, slightly confused, but started pulling things out of the basket. He had prepared chicken salad sandwiches (the absolute best I'd ever tasted – he wouldn't give me the recipe), asparagus spears which had been blanched to perfection, and cubed cheese with crackers. It was the perfect amount of food.

"I hope you don't mind asparagus." He said. "It's one of my favorites and I was really craving it today for some reason."

Oh dear. "No, I don't mind it. Actually, it's one of my favorites too."

"Really?" Lance looked at me incredulously. "Wow! Most people don't mind it but hardly anyone ever says it's their favorite, even if they don't mind it. You're not just saying that because I said it's my favorite, right?"

"Right."

"So you really *do* like it?"

"Yes!" I was started to get annoyed with the entire evening. It was perfect. *Why does it have to be perfect, Lord? I could handle it if it was less than perfect.*

"Very cool!" Lance's head bobbed up and down. Our eyes met and we both stopped. I could feel my resolve melting even more under his gaze but I couldn't look away. After what seemed an eternity Lance looked down, "Well, I guess I should get all this picked up before the music starts." He began packing the containers in the picnic basket.

Lord, You know where I stand. I want You to be my best friend. I don't need..... I gulped. I don't need Lance, or any guy, to fulfill me in any way. My happiness is in You, God. Please help me to be able to just be friends here and not make things any more awkward. I need you a lot right now, God. Help me?

I took a deep breath before speaking. "So...." Lance looked up quickly with an expectant look in his face.

"Yeah?" His gaze urged me to speak. I'd been pretty quiet since arriving at the park.

"Um." I tried to think of something to say. Nothing was coming to me.

Lance rescued me. Again. "So where are you from, Nel?"

We spent the rest of our time before the music began talking about me. It was not as awkward as I thought it would be; Lance had a way about him that put me completely at ease. I was going to have a harder time than I thought putting him off.

As the last note was played and people began picking up and making their way to their cars, I heard a heavy sigh. I glanced over to find Lance with his knees drawn up toward his chest and his elbows resting on them, his chin resting in his left hand. He had a far-away look in his eyes.

"What's wrong?" *I knew I'd been quiet but had he really had that horrible of a time?*

He looked at me with a slight smile tugging at the corners of his mouth. "I wish it wasn't over just yet."

"But it's almost 9:30, Lance. If it went much longer I think I'd fall asleep right here."

"That's not what I'm talking about." He shook his head and looked down, that goofy grin finding its way to his lips.

"Well, I'm not sure."

"I'm not ready to take you back yet, okay?" Lance jumped to his feet and jerked at the blanket on which I was still seated.

I jumped up and crossed my arms, "Well, for not wanting to take me back you're sure in a hurry!" *What's his problem? Boys are so strange.*

"Hey," he said, the corners of his mouth curling up in a smile. "How 'bout let's get ice cream!"

Oh my soul. He just hit another soft spot!

I woke up Sunday morning with a smile on my face. I had enjoyed my date with Lance a bit more than I maybe should have, and I didn't feel as guilty as I thought I should. *Lord, what's going on with me? I tried not to have too much fun but I really did enjoy myself. It can't be bad to just be friends, right? He'd understand that. Right?* I wasn't sure I wanted to tell Lance the real reason that I couldn't go on a second date. I knew myself and I knew that if I allowed myself to spend much more time alone with him that I would grow more attached than I ought to be.

Lance had asked on the way home from the concert if he could sit with me in church the next morning and I had said yes without thinking. I knew I couldn't get out of seeing him. I was going to need some extra help today keeping my heart under control. I reached for my Bible on my nightstand and let it fall open. My eyes fell on an underlined verse, it was *Jeremiah 24:7, "And I will give them an heart to know me, that I am the Lord: and they shall be my people, and I will be their God: for they shall return unto me with their whole heart."* That was exactly what I needed to hear. I needed to be focused on knowing God, not on getting into a relationship. No matter how much I enjoyed spending time with Lance, we could never be anything more than friends until my heart was wholly God's.

CHAPTER 10

S unday morning came way too quickly! I did not want to go to church -- at least not the Straight Paths Baptist Church. After reality had set in, I realized what a horrible mistake it had been saying yes to Lance.

What was I thinking when I agreed to sit with Lance in church?

There was no way out! *Wait...* I felt my forehead.

"Tam!" I called from the kitchen as I brewed a fresh pot of java.

"Boy, that smells good Nel," Tam said as she rubbed the sleep from her eyes. "What's up?"

"I don't feel so well Tam. I think I'm running a fever."

"Let me see," Tam said as she placed her hand on my forehead. "I don't think so Nel… what have you got yourself into now?"

"Are you sure I don't have a fever?"

"Sure I'm sure you don't have a fever, and I'm sure you've got yourself into another mess! Who is it this time? Let me guess -- Lance? What did he do now? No, wait... let me rephrase that. What did *you* do now?"

"Oh Tam. Last night he asked me if I would sit next to him in church today, and I said yes without even thinking!"

"You go girl!" Tam shrieked.

"No Tam! Seriously, what am I going to do?"

"You're going to take a shower, slide into that pretty little pink sundress you have, and… wait a sec.." She ran into her room and came out with a small Victoria's Secret bag.

No way!

"And you're gonna splash some of this *Dream Angels Heavenly Summer* perfume I got ya!" she said grinning from ear to ear.

"Now get going. You can wait on the Lord, but don't make Lance wait on you!"

Tam and Donel were going with me to church. I was torn about that. Part of me wanted the moral support, the other part of me thought, *where there's Tam, there is usually drama,* and I did not need any more drama!

Donel arrived punctually, as usual, and we headed to the coffee shop. I wasn't anxious about Lance so much as I was about facing Nic Spaulding after my abrupt departure from the coffee shop.

What would I say? What should I say? Maybe he's already forgotten. No way… not a chance. He doesn't seem like the forgetting type!

"Nelia Lynn Chambers! What on earth are you spacing out about now? Donel has asked you three times what you're having!"

A horn honked behind us. I jumped. "Hurry, hurry!"

"Give me a strawberry and cream frappuccino," I said thinking *I'm already on edge. More caffeine would do me in!*

As we pulled away from the drive-thru window, Tam turned and handed me my beverage, and said, "Take a real deep breath and slowly let it out. That's what I do to cleanse my mind."

Oh brother! What works for you Tam doesn't work for me… ever!

I was really losing it. After all, Tam was my roommate and friend, and despite her glamorous appearance, I loved her dearly.

Lance was waiting for me in the foyer when we arrived at church. Donel and Lance shook hands and Tam stepped in between them and gave Lance a big hug. "How are you doing Lance?"

"Fine, and you?"

"Great!"

Without taking a breath she continued, "doesn't Nel look fantastic?"

Lance looked at me and suddenly my knees felt weak.

"Yes. You look fantastic Nel," he said turning to me with open arms. We hugged awkwardly.

"And you smell... how do I put this? Heavenly!"

I turned as I felt my face flush and hurried into the sanctuary. "We need to sit down."

We sat down about ten rows from the pulpit. Me, Lance, and Tamara, with Donel closest to the aisle. The pews felt more cushy than the previous week. *Could it be that sitting next to Lance made them feel softer?*

Lord help me! Satan has followed me right into this sanctuary and is playing mind games with me, I thought. I felt a panic attack coming on.

"Pssst, pssst." I looked up and two rows in front of me sat Sandi and Jim. Sandi had turned around and was trying to get my attention. With a big smile she mouthed the words, *We're glad you're here.*

I smiled back nervously and whispered, "Thank you.".

The song leader stepped up to the pulpit as Nic walked onto the stage and took a seat. The chatter turned to whispers and then the congregation became silent as the song leader said, "Turn in your hymnals to page 176."

Looking over his spectacles at the congregants, the song leader raised his left hand and began.

Some glad morning when this life is o'er,
I'll fly away To a home on God's celestial shore,
I'll fly away

I couldn't believe my ears! By the time the chorus began, I knew I must be dreaming. Lance had the most beautiful tenor voice; each note rolled off his lips with such clarity. And he had not even *opened* the hymnal!

What else could be so perfect yet so wrong for me at the same time?

By the time the song service ended and Nic got up to preach, I was finally feeling at ease. The combination of Lance's angelic voice and simply being in the house of the Lord had rid me of most of my anxiety.

Nic began with a heartwarming prayer:

"Lord, Creator of the heavens and the earth, Father of all mankind. We come to you today with humble hearts asking your blessing upon this service and upon this message. Lord, let us not be tricked into the world's ways. Let us trust solely in you and your Word because we know it to be the Truth. Give us the courage to not only live it but share it with others. In Jesus name we pray. Amen."

"Many of you today will feel like I am speaking directly to you. In preparing this lesson, I know my own toes felt stepped on pretty bad!" Nic chuckled.

"The idea came to me when I was in Borders last week looking for a good book to read. I went to a shelf and grabbed the book with the best looking cover, and I walked over and plopped down in one of those overstuffed chairs and began to read."

He paused momentarily.

"And you know what?"

"What?" I blurted out.

Pastors tend to ask rhetorical questions often, but I was caught up in the moment. I felt my face flush.

Nic took it in stride, looked directly at me, smiled, and said, "I'm glad you asked."

"The book was awful! I read three or four pages and I had to put it down. I wanted a good book so I went back to the shelf and picked one with a snappy title and sat down with it. And you know what?"

He looked at me and smiled again. "Nel's not falling for that again!" The congregation laughed.

"That book wasn't so good either. Turn in your bibles to *Matthew 7* and read along with me."

I knew that scripture well.

"Judge not, that ye be not judged. For with what judgment ye judge, ye shall be judged: and with what measure ye mete, it shall be measured to you again. And why beholdest thou the mote that is in thy brother's eye, but considerest not the beam that is in thine own eye? Or how wilt thou say to thy brother, Let me pull out the mote out of thine eye; and, behold, a beam is in thine own eye? Thou hypocrite, first cast out the beam out of thine own eye; and then shalt thou see clearly to cast out the mote out of thy brother's eye."

I thought *if there was ever a time in my life that a sermon was meant for me, this had to be it!*

From the time we had sat down in the sanctuary, Lance perceived that I had my boundaries and didn't scoot over close or put his arm around me. Occasionally throughout the service, he would glance at me and smile.

The invitation song was *I Surrender All.*

Once again God was trying to get my attention and Satan was trying to lure me into Lance's arms with that beautiful tenor voice.

Nic greeted each of us as we filed out of the sanctuary. He took my hand with both of his and said, "Thanks Nel for the help today. You were great!"

Well now I'm confused Lord. He seemed so sincere. Was that the same Nic you had in Your pulpit last Sunday?

As we exited the building, Lance said, "See you sometime this week?"

"Sure. I have to have my caffeine fix."

"Alright then. Later!" he said, his head bobbing up and down as he grinned and gave me a salute.

Well that is both a disappointment and a relief.

Tamara said, "Donel and I will drop you off at home on our way to Granite Bay."

"Oh that's right. I forgot you have that fashion show fundraiser thingy."

As I was getting into Donel's Land Rover, Sandi and Jim were exiting the building. "Nelia! Wait!" Sandi yelled as she stumbled across the grass in her high heels.

"We planned on having you for lunch today. Come on. You can ride with me. Jim went with Lee already to get the barbeque started."

How do I get out of this? It's probably best to just get it over with.

"Okay. I'll see you later Tam. Drive safe Donel."

Shortly after we arrived at Sandi and Jim's home, Nic showed up. I was expecting him, and planned to be pleasant with him, but not overly friendly.

Jim had laid out a nice buffet out back on the patio. Barbecued ribs, corn on the cob, and watermelon, and Lee was turning an old hand crank ice cream machine making fresh apricot ice cream.

Before I knew it, I was letting my hair down, talking and laughing, and just having fun! I had forgotten Lance for the time being and was finding Nic to be quite charming. He had taken his coat off and loosened his tie, and when he took his finger and wiped some barbeque sauce from the corner of my mouth I thought *this could work out.*

The afternoon went by quick and Nic asked me if I would like a ride back to church.

"Sure," I said feeling more and more comfortable. *After all he is a pastor. That is my type.*

I enjoyed the evening service. It was more relaxed than the morning service and so was I!

After the service I waited for Nic as he locked up the church. It was chilly outside and he took his jacket off and put it around my shoulders.

We rode the few short blocks to my apartment in silence. He walked me to my door and said, "Nel, I really had a great time today. Thank you!"

I simply said, "Likewise." I smiled at him and he smiled back, and I turned and went into my apartment.

I washed my face and brushed my teeth and then I sat down with Figaro. "What do you think, buddy?"

Meow!

"Oh that's what you said last time!"

I was asleep when Tam got home, and she was asleep when I went to work.

I had two cups of coffee before I left the apartment and figured that would be enough caffeine to get me to the office. I wanted to avoid the coffee shop for a few days to see if my feelings for Lance would pass.

When I arrived at work, I was bombarded with questions from Jim and Sandi about what I thought about Pastor Nic. The phone began ringing off the hook though, like every Monday morning, and soon everyone was busy at work. I worked right through lunch fielding calls, so at 3 o'clock Jim said, "Nelia, you can go home. I'll close up shop."

"Thanks Jim, but I don't mind staying."

"I know, but you've worked hard. Go on now, before I change my mind!"

I went straight home, hoping to find Tam there so I could tell her about my Sunday afternoon.

She was sitting on the couch painting her toenails *hot pink*. I looked at Figaro who was curled up alongside her, his front paw sticking out revealing his *hot pink* claws.

"Mommy came home to save you from Tam's insanity, but it looks like mommy's too late!

"Wow. You're in a great mood! What gives?"

"Well.." The doorbell rang.

"Oh that's probably Donel. I left my cell phone in his car."

I opened the door and a young guy with a dozen red roses in an ornate vase said, "I have a delivery for Nelia Lynn Chambers."

"That's me," I said feeling perplexed.

"Just need you to sign here."

I took the clipboard and signed on the dotted line. The delivery guy handed me the flowers, took his clipboard, and before he turned to go said, "Look's like somebody's in love."

I turned around to find Tam facing me her mouth gaping open. "Who are they from? I bet Lance!"

I set the vase down on the kitchen table and sat down to open the card that was attached. My hands trembled as I tore at the envelope.

"Read it. Read it Nel!"

I read it to myself. *I can't believe this. This isn't happening to me!*

"The suspense is killing me Nel!"

"Okay Okay! It says 'I'll be in San Francisco next week for a job interview with Chase Bank. Hope we can spend some time together. I've missed you so much. Brian.'"

CHAPTER 11

I sat stunned and even Tam stood perfectly still without saying a word.

I had not heard from Brian in over three years. *Why now? What does he want?*

Brian and I had broken up while I was still in college. He was three years older than I and had a way with words; he knew just what to say to manipulate and control me. While we had been dating I had done things of which I was not proud and I suddenly felt the same intense guilt and anxiety sweeping over me as I had felt when we were together. I hadn't given myself wholly to Brian, but I had allowed him more freedom than I should have.

Why does he have to show up now, God? I don't know if I can take this! Are you judging me because I've been thinking about the possibility of a relationship? I'm sorry, okay?! I really am trying to just be friends with Lance and Nic, I promise! I'll never speak to another guy again if You'll just make Brian go away! Just make it all stop.

I was shaking and short of breath. Tam sat down next to me and wrapped her arms around my neck. "It'll be okay, Nel. We'll figure something out."

Tuesday seemed to drag by as each minute brought me that much closer to the possibility of having to face Brian again. I had no idea what I was going to do. Tam was unusually quiet as well and I could tell my predicament was affecting her nearly as much as it was affecting me.

Wednesday morning we walked into Starbucks and Lance called out from behind the counter, "G'morning, ladies! What's crack-a-lackin'?"

I couldn't bring myself to reply. Tam answered with a half-hearted, "Hey, Lance."

Lance looked perplexed but went about making a vanilla latte for the man waiting impatiently at the end of the counter. It was our turn to order. Tam ordered what she wanted without any of her usual indecision and I ordered a caramel macchiato with a single shot of espresso – I knew I needed the caffeine but if I got too much, it would only make my jitters worse.

"Just one shot, Nel?" Lance teased. "You know if you always just get a single shot you'll always be single, right? It's like the caffeine-aholic curse," he explained with a chuckle.

"Fine by me." I mumbled.

Lance finished making our drinks in silence and waited for us at the end of the counter. Tam grabbed hers and headed for the door without so much as a 'bye' to Lance. As I reached for my macchiato he pulled it back and leaned forward over the counter, "What's going on, Nel?" he asked in a quiet voice.

"Nothing. Can I just have my drink." I didn't make eye contact.

Lance stared at me, waiting for an explanation. When I didn't offer anything more he said, "Nel, I can see something's wrong. It's nothing I said or did, right? 'Cause if I did anything that offended you or hurt you in any way I'd give anything to take it back."

"No, no. It's not you."

"Then, what?" he pleaded. "You can tell me."

I hesitated for only a moment. "I can't. I have to go to work, Lance. May I have my drink?" I reached across the counter, waiting for him to hand me my coffee. I felt bad when I saw the hurt look on his face but I really had no choice.

He wouldn't understand. I thought. *Then again, maybe he would. He's probably the same way!* Something inside me told me that was not true, but it made me feel better to think that all guys fell into the same category at the moment; it was easier.

Lance handed me my coffee but held on to it for a brief moment. "I'm praying for you, Nelia."

My breath caught in my throat. I couldn't move. *What on earth? Why did he just say that? God? Help?* When I didn't respond, Lance let my cup go and turned to make another drink. I stood there for a second, stunned. I was so confused. *He doesn't even know what's going on. He can't honestly mean that.*

"Nel!" I spun on my heel. Tam stood in the doorway looking frustrated. "Let's go! We'll both be late!"

I hurried to the door. Glancing over my shoulder I caught one last glimpse of Lance. I'd never seen him so serious and focused on making a drink before. I felt a strange twinge in my heart. *What's going on with me, God?* It was like something deep within me was craving one last glance, one quick flash of a smile from Lance, and when I didn't get it, my problem seemed so much bigger.

I let out a deep heartfelt sigh and hurried to the car. This week was feeling longer and longer.

By the time 6 o'clock rolled around I knew I needed some serious time with God. My day had gone from bad to worse . After the conversation with Lance had left me reeling that morning, I had received a text from Brian saying *I can't wait to see you. We really need to talk, babe. Lots to tell.*

What's that supposed to mean? It ate at me all day. I decided the only thing to do was go to church. I remembered how that had always been the thing to give me that extra boost to make it through the rest of the week until Sunday. I glanced at my watch. 6:15. I had just enough time to run home and freshen up before driving the few blocks to Straight Paths.

In just the few visits I had made to Straight Paths Baptist Church it already felt somewhat like home. The people were friendly, the songs were the same I had sung growing up, and the pastor, well what could I say about him? His messages were pretty brief compared to what I grew up hearing, but they cut right to the heart. He was obviously in touch with God, because God was definitely using him in the pulpit.

I rushed home and flew into my bedroom.

Tam came running in, "What's going on? Are you okay? Brian didn't show up did he? Why are you flustered?!" She was standing in the middle of my bedroom fanning herself with both hands franticly.

"Nothing is wrong, Tam." I chuckled. "I just decided I'm going to church tonight and I have to hurry if I'm gonna make it on time." I grabbed my brush and started running it through my hair.

"Church?" Tam looked puzzled, as if the thought of attending church mid-week was something she'd never heard before now.

"Yes, church. I think I could use a dose of preaching right now."

"I wanna come too!" Tam rushed out of my bedroom as fast as she'd come.

Well, that's a first! I could use the company though. "You have to hurry, Tam! We'll be late!"

Tam took her sweet time and we were a few minutes late. As we walked into the back of the sanctuary Nic was beginning to open the service in prayer. We snuck into a pew near the back and I found myself sitting next to the same old lady I sat next to on my first visit to Straight Paths. She was wearing the same hat she'd worn that first Sunday. She peeked when she heard us shuffle in and moved down the pew a bit to make room.

"Good to see you again, love." She whispered and winked at me.

"Thanks. You too." I whispered back and smiled.

Nic ended the prayer and we all sat down. Tam and I realized at the same time that we had both forgotten our bibles. I was embarrassed. *Never in my life have I forgotten to bring my Bible to church! What's gotten into me?*

The passage was announced and the lady next to me noticed our empty hands. She handed me her Bible and said, "I can share with my daughter."

I saw a lady in her mid-40's peek around the lady. She looked like a mirror image of the hat lady. She smiled and nodded at me.

"Thank you." I whispered as I took the Bible. The pages were marked with tear stains and notes had been carefully written in the margins. Clearly this woman loved this Book.

The passage was *Hebrews* 11. *The Hall of Faith.* I remembered my dad calling it that when I was growing up. This chapter was full of people who did amazing things for God simply because they had faith. Nic began to read in verse thirty.

"*30 By faith the walls of Jericho fell down, after they were compassed about seven days. 31 By faith the harlot Rahab perished not with them that believed not, when she had received the spies with peace. 32 And what shall I more say? For the time would fail me to tell of Gedeon, and of Barak, and of Samson, and of Jephthae; of David also, and Samuel, and of the prophets: 33 Who through faith subdued kingdoms, wrought righteousness, obtained promises, stopped the mouths of lions, 34 Quenched the violence of fire, escaped the edge of the sword, out of weakness were made strong, waxed valiant in fight, turned to flight the armies of the aliens.*"

He stopped there and paused. There was a hush over the congregation as we all waited for him speak. When he did, he did so softly and almost hesitantly.

"My friends," he took a deep breath. "I'm not sure why God's telling me to talk about this passage tonight. This was not the passage I had prepared to speak from earlier today as I studied for tonight. This isn't even the passage I was thinking of as we sang a moment ago. But God obviously has a reason for it."

I could feel the hum of the other congregants as people wondered quietly what God would give the pastor tonight.

"I want us to think about some of the people mentioned in this chapter; this *Hall of Faith* if you will. We find people like Abraham, Moses, Isaac, Jacob, Noah, Abel, and even Enoch who never died; God just took him straight to Heaven and skipped that step because he pleased God so well." Nic took a moment to gather his thoughts, his brow creased. "But then we also find people like David who had an affair and even had a man murdered. Sara is mentioned and she laughed at God in her heart when she heard she was going to have a child in her old age. We find at the end of the chapter a most surprising name. That name is Rahab, the harlot."

I stared at the page in front of me. I couldn't believe it. Why had I not noticed this before?

"God recognized the faith of this woman, in spite of who she was and in spite of everything she had ever done. It did not matter to God."

I could feel the tears start to roll down my cheeks.

"How did Rahab end up here mingled with these spiritual giants? What kind of price did she have to pay to be listed here? Simple. It wasn't gold or silver. There was no exchange of merchandise or services. The answer is faith." Nic stepped back from the pulpit, his hands in his pockets, looking out over the congregation. No one was speaking; you could hear sniffles from around the room as the truth of what Nic was saying began to sink into the hearts of the hearers.

"This woman had nothing of physical value or worth to offer. All that she had was her heart. She realized that nothing she did could outweigh what God had done for her and she placed her faith in the God of heaven, the only One who could ever outweigh all her sin. Friends, it's never an even balance when God gets involved. He puts his blood on the one side and nothing we can ever do, good or bad, will ever outweigh Him. Rahab was a harlot, and she is forever remembered as a harlot but in God's eyes she was a spiritual giant just like Moses and Abraham and Enoch. In *Psalm 51*, the Psalm of David, after the prophet, Nathan, came and pointed out his sin with Bathsheba, David says in verse 10, '*Create in me a clean heart, O God; and renew a right spirit within me.*' David got it right, folks." Nic waited to let the truth sink in.

"David got it right." He said again quietly. "I think tonight we all need to take a minute, or an hour, whatever it takes, and make some things right with God. I know tonight I haven't brought the house down with some dynamic message, but this is what God gave me, folks; it must be right. We need to realize that no matter what we've done or what we struggle with, God's already paid for it. He's already got the victory over our past, present, and even our future… We just have to claim it! It's not our place to fight the battles; we just need to trust God like in the battle of Jericho. Whatever you have done, friend, whatever you are struggling with right now, give it to God. Allow Him to do a work in your heart you never imagined possible. Allow Him to create a new heart in you and to renew your spirit. You'll be surprised what having just a little bit of faith on your part will give way to God doing great things in your life. Let's all just bow our heads and spend time with God. You talk to God as long as you need and as you finish just go ahead and leave quietly. I'll be in the back if anyone wants me to pray with them."

With that, Nic walked to lobby and left the congregation to pray silently. Some people went forward to the altar while many remained in their seats with their heads bowed. I wept like I'd not wept before.

God, you knew I needed to hear this tonight. You know my heart, Abba. You know the guilt I've been feeling for allowing Brian to take liberties with me when we were dating and, God, I am tired of trying to bare this weight alone! I need your help. Please forgive me for being weak and not giving You full control. Abba, You're my God. You know me. You know my weaknesses and my struggles. Please, Father, help me to trust you and to bring these things to You each and every day – every time I feel myself being tempted away from You. I want to be who You want me to be, not who I want me to be or who Brian wants me to be. Help me to find my identity in You and to feel complete with You and You alone. Give me the strength to stand up to Brian and tell him the Truth, God. I know I can't do it on my own, but I can if I just trust You. God, I need wisdom.

I didn't know what else to pray so I just sat there quietly, thinking. So much of what had happened could have been avoided if my relationship with God had been right all along. I had caused myself so much heartache by being foolish. I realized now that, in spite of my weakness and foolishness, God desired to empower me with His strength if only I would trust Him – like Rahab.

It was not going to be easy, but I knew what I had to do.

CHAPTER 12

Tamara must have felt a strong conviction. I wasn't sure. I didn't care. All I know is that the silence, as we began the short journey home, was deafening.

What? I didn't care?

"That's one of your problems Nel. You only care about yourself. Maybe you need to reread that Max Lucado book *It's Not About Me.*" God was speaking to me again. Not in a little voice in my head – a big voice – a big booming voice!

I said that about Nic.

"What happened to the Nel that used to be so on fire to share My Word, the Truth with the whole world? You were going to tell Lance about your commitment to Me, but did you mention Me? Do you even know if Lance knows the Truth? Has Satan robbed you of the abilities I gave you?"

I began to feel sick to my stomach. *I get it Lord! I get it!*

"That's what you said a few weeks ago when I assured you that I was the Friend that would always be there for you. Remember tonight's sermon Nel. Remember your Dad talking about the *Hall of Faith*, and remember I will never desert you."

Enough Lord! I really DO get it! I realized my nausea was driven by my guilt and shame.

"I'm not through Nel. Your roommate Tamara… she's watching you."

What? I hadn't thought of that.

"I know you understand what I'm saying Nel. Tamara has a desire to know me, but she doesn't KNOW know me yet. That's where you come in. You're my ambassador."

I took my eyes off the road momentarily to steal a glance at my roommate. *She looks so perfect.*

"That's just one of Satan's many tricks. He makes her *look* perfect. It's an illusion Nel. Only I can MAKE her perfect through the blood of the Lamb."

Gosh. I never looked at it that way.

"You are one of Mine Nel. But you still have a lot to learn." He said to me as I parked in front of our apartment.

"You timed this conversation to end just as I pulled up in front of the apartment," I said softly.

"What?" Tam said sleepily as the car came to a halt.

"That was amazing!"

"What? What did I miss?"

"I'll tell you later!"

Tam went straight to bed when we walked in the door. I was exhausted but at the same time energized by God's chat with me on the ride home.

I put on a pot of coffee and fed Figaro who was skirting around my legs with his tail high in the air like a flag flying high. He was growing fast, but still cute as ever.

When the coffee was made, I poured the robust Caffè Verona into my smiley face mug, went into my room, and sat on my bed. I contemplated grabbing my calendar; late night was for planning. I was all about planning and lists. If everything was not meticulously planned, nothing worked. This time, I grabbed my Bible instead.

I opened the Book to a familiar passage. *Matthew* Chapter 6, skimmed the verses and stopped at verse 24. I began reading.

No man can serve two masters: for either he will hate the one, and love the other; or else he will hold to the one, and despise the other. Ye cannot serve God and mammon.

I began to study this verse. I wanted to know the *meaning* of this – God's Word – *today*, in my life!

I knew mammon meant money, but I also remembered debates in Sunday School over whether or not the word mammon may have a bigger implication, not just money but *all* worldly things.

Could He be telling me that my desire for a relationship could be viewed as mammon? And that it had become my master?

The picture was becoming much clearer. *I'm seeing Lord. Open my eyes some more.*

I read on:

25 Therefore I say unto you, Take no thought for your life, what ye shall eat, or what ye shall drink; nor yet for your body, what ye shall put on. Is not the life more than meat, and the body than raiment? 26 Behold the fowls of the air: for they sow not, neither do they reap, nor gather into barns; yet your heavenly Father feedeth them. Are ye not much better than they?

I know all that stuff Lord. Those verses have been drilled into me since I was knee-high to a grasshopper. Oh, but wait. Yes I hear you… I've been worrying about other things, like guys!

I continued reading:

27 Which of you by taking thought can add one cubit unto his stature?

You know God, if I could, I would make myself at least five foot six, because I don't do well in heels. Yeah, that was a good one Lord.

I skimmed a couple of verses and stopped on verse 30:

Wherefore, if God so clothe the grass of the field, which today is, and tomorrow is cast into the oven, shall he not much more clothe you, O ye of little faith?

O ye of little faith... That cut me like a knife! I read the last part again, out loud. "O, ye of little faith?"

I read it again; this time the words caught in my throat. I took a sip of coffee and flipped over to *Hebrews 11*. There it was, verse 31. My body began to tremble. It was like two pieces of a puzzle fitting together perfectly... I had stopped at verse 30 of *Matthew* Chapter 6.

I held my finger at that place and flipped back to *Hebrews* Chapter 11 and yes. There was the perfect verse to follow. Verse 31! I read it out loud. "By faith the harlot Rahab perished not with them that believed not, when she had received the spies with peace."

I savored it like I savored my coffee.

I knew the key to having faith like the harlot Rahab was only a couple verses away. They were highlighted numerous times with various colors. The verse was barely visible, but I knew it and it was to be my new mantra!

But seek ye first the kingdom of God, and his righteousness; and all these things shall be added unto you.

I could hardly sleep that night, partly due to high levels of caffeine flowing through my veins, but mainly due to the transformation I was feeling.

I was dressed and ready to go to work by 7:00 a.m. when Tamara came out of her room rubbing the sleep from her eyes.

"Good morning!" I said. "It's such a beautiful morning."

"What are you up to?" Tam asked as she stretched and yawned.

"Just feeling great! Can I get you a cup of coffee?"

"Sure. But first tell me what you did with my friend Nel."

"Ha ha. You're so funny Tam! I just loooove having you as my roomie," I said as I hugged her. I handed my smiley face cup filled with fresh brewed coffee.

"Oh no! You're not Nel! Nel would never let anyone drink out of *her* cup. What have you done with her? Does this have anything to do with last night. Did the rapture happen while I was sleeping?"

"No silly. It's me for real. Ask me anything that you would ask Nel and I my answer will prove that I am Nel!"

"What are you going to do about Brian?"

Oh brother!

I hadn't thought about Brian, or Lance, or Nic, but I had to decide what to do, what to say when Brian called. He would be in San Francisco next week. I didn't have a lot of time to think about it or pray about it.

To say that the caffiene had me moving fast would be an understatement. I scurried around the office tidying others' desks, emptying trash cans, grabbing the phone before the first ring had barely sounded. I hadn't noticed everyone standing around with gaping mouths until Sandi grabbed my arm as I scooted around her to grab Jim's waste basket all the while humming *There's Power in the Blood*.

"What has gotten into you Nel?"

"Oh nothing… just having a *great* day!"

"Could it have anything to do with Pastor Nic's lesson last night? You know, the Lord used him in a mighty way last night."

"Maybe," I said in a sing-songy way.

Jim and Sandi both gave me a puzzled look as I walked out of the office with a definite bounce in my step!

The rest of the day zinged past, and before I knew it, the time was five o'clock. I texted Tam - *Meet me 4 coffee.*

Her response was immediate as if she was waiting to here from me. *Do u need n e mor caffiene? Lol*

Haha I want 2 talk 2 lance.

k

As I walked into the coffee shop, I heard squealing tires. I turned to see Tam rounding the corner into the parking lot in Donel's Land Rover. The passenger side wheels barely touched the ground, and I could see Tam leaning fierciously toward the center of the SUV.

I was halfway through the door but turned and walked outside to meet Tam. She was wild-eyed, a very different Tam than I was used to.

"Does Donel know you drive his baby like that?

"No, but I had to be here to see this."

"See what?"

"What's about to happen between you and Lance!" She blew a bubble with her gum and smiled.

"Nothings about to happen. I just wanted to get a caramel macchiato and thought you would like to join me and…"

"Flirt with Lance. I know you like him Nel. You can't hide it!"

"It ain't like that Tam!"

Lance came out of the stock room wiping his hands on his apron. "What brings you two lovely ladies to this establishment this fine afternoon? I betcha planned this... seeing as it's my breaktime. You just came to chill with me *right mates?*" The Australian accent at the end made me chuckle. His head bopped up and down as he smiled and pulled out two chairs simultaneously. "Have a seat *me lovely ladies.*"

His look then turned serious. "I need to talk to you Nel. I need to ask you a favor."

"Sure Lance. What is it?"

He glanced at Tam momentarily.

"Would you like me to leave? Give you a little privacy *big boy?*"

"No. It's nothing like that. You're welcome to stay."

Donel walked in the door with a couple of his coworkers. Tam spotted them, got up, and rushed over to greet Donel.

"This is better," Lance said. "Tam seems like a lot of fun, but I really enjoy *your* company. Yep Nelia, I really like you."

I'm quite comfortable with you, I thought. Lance was becoming like that old pair of sneakers. You know, the ones you want to get rid of but you can't bring yourself to do it because they *feel* so good.

"There you go again Nel?"

I shook my head as I came out of my trance.

"You sure zone out a lot when you're with me."

"I'm sorry. Go ahead. What was the favor you wanted to ask?"

"They put me on the schedule next Tuesday until closing. Amanda goes for her therapy at Stanford. She has to be there all afternoon, and well.. Would you go with her?"

"Sure. I can take the day off. I'm sure Jim will let me."

"Oh thank you Nel. Thank you soooo much."

"Do you think I can get her wheelchair in the back of my car?

"Oh no. You don't have to worry about that. Amanda will drive."

"Amanda *drives*?"

"Of course she does. We have a specially equiped Durango with hand controls and everything."

"You mean the accelerator and brakes and all are controlled by Amanda's hands?"

"Nelia, Nelia. Have you been living in another world. Amanda does lots of things. She even swims."

"No way!"

"Yes, way. Matter of fact, she loves to swim!"

"How does she do it? I mean, with her legs paralyzed."

"You should know that Nelia. With God all things are possible, O ye of little faith!" He chuckled and put both palms out in front of him. "Just kidding."

"I guess I don't know much about people living with physical disablities," I said with a disconcerted look.

"They're just like you and me Nelia. They have emotions and feelings just like you and me and they have fears and doubts just like you and me. Which brings me to the real reason I would like you to accompany my little sister to Stanford."

"And what is that?"

"You haven't seen her at church have you?"

"No. I just assumed it was hard for her to get out and about."

"Well, the reason you haven't seen Amanda at church is not unbelief, but it's close to it. Since she has been going to Stanford, a lot of questions have been raised in her mind about God's existance."

"So how can I help?"

"She doesn't want to listen to me anymore. Soooo… I thought… well, she likes you… and you're smart. Plus I can tell you love the Lord."

Wow! That was a huge compliment, but my actions really hadn't demonstrated that. Why would he say that?

"Well thanks for the compliments, undeserved as they may be. I'll find a way to talk to her, share with her some of my own struggles… yeah Lance. It'll be fun getting to know your sister and prying some of your little secrets out of her!"

"Gotta get back to work. See ya Nelia. Thanks a bunch!"

I felt good about recognizing an opportunity that God had placed before me. I arrived home before Tam. The phone was ringing as I walked through the door. I looked for the handset and spotted the flashing light between the cushions on the couch. I answered without checking the caller I.D.

"Hello?"

"Hi Nelia. Oh it's so great to hear your voice."

"Brian?"

"Yes babe, it's me. I called to tell you I am arriving in San Francisco Monday morning. My interview's in the afternoon. I am free all day Tuesday. Do you think I can come and see you?"

"Well actually Brian, I'm…"

Brian cut me off, "I won't take no! I've gotta see you babe!"

He hadn't changed a bit.

"Well if you would let me finish."

"Sorry babe. Go ahead."

"I have to go to Stanford Tuesday afternoon. Can we meet in the city for lunch?"

"Perfect!"

"Oh and Brian."

"Yeah babe?"

"I'll have a friend with me. See you Tuesday. Gotta go. Bye."

I disconnected, looked up and said, "Thank you Lord!"

CHAPTER 13

I walked into Starbucks Friday morning hoping to catch Lance during a slow time. I hadn't had a chance to talk to him about what I really wanted to talk about the day before because he'd bombarded me with the conversation about Amanda. As I entered the coffee shop, I could tell right away there was no way he'd be able to chat. The line of people waiting to order wrapped all the way around the tables and ended just two feet inside the door. The same amount of people seemed to be waiting for their drinks to be made. I tried to catch his eye but Lance was hurriedly making drink after drink and making small talk with customers to keep them occupied while he whipped up their orders.

Ah well. Maybe later, I thought.

I decided I could drink office coffee instead of Starbucks today. *Oh! I hope Lee didn't make it this morning. Drinking his coffee is like drinking coffee flavored water. Yuck!* I rushed to the office and walked in just as Lee was pouring water in the back of the coffee pot.

"G'mornin', lady!" he greeted me with a huge grin. *Classic Lee.*

"Good morning, Lee." I looked longingly at the coffee pot. *If only I'd been two minutes earlier!*

Just then Lee's phone rang. "Oh! Gotta answer that, Nel. Would you mind….?" He pointed to the coffee pot.

"Not at all!"

Thank you, Jesus!

I added two more scoops of coffee, finished pouring the water, and pressed the on button. Soon, the office filled with the rich scent of strong coffee. I sat at my desk and listened to the hum of business around me. Nothing felt the same. My entire perspective seemed to have changed since Wednesday night. I could tell that I was different. I felt happier and I had a peace inside that had been missing from my life for a long time. I bowed my head.

Lord, I don't even know where to start. Thank You! Yeah…. That's all. Just, thanks!

Friday seemed to fly by. Sandi had been hinting around all week, trying to figure out who Lance was and why I had been sitting next to him in church. By Friday she had pretty much given up and gone back to singing the praises of Nic Spaulding. I still was unsure about him. I'd gotten such different vibes from him with each encounter and wasn't exactly sure who he really was. Perhaps I would have a chance this weekend to get to know him a bit more.

Saturday morning rolled around earlier than usual. I woke up at 5:00 a.m. and crawled out of bed. I'm one of those people who, once I'm awake, I can't go back to sleep. I padded my way into the kitchen and put on a pot of my favorite coffee – *Fog Cutter* by *Alakef Coffee,* a company back home. Tam thought I was crazy for ordering my coffee online, but it was *so* worth it, and she didn't complain at all when she was drinking it by the pot.

I filled my cup and snuggled into my overstuffed armchair to read my Bible. As I contemplated where to read today I noticed a piece of paper sticking out between the pages and opened to the passage it was marking. I realized it was the place I had left off reading several years ago when I had been trying to read through the Bible in one year.

What better place to pick up reading than right where I left off?

The paper had been holding my place in the book of *Ezra*. I began reading in Chapter one and couldn't seem to stop. I was so wrapped up in the story that I was to Chapter 10 before I realized I had read so much. I stopped at chapter 10, verse 1. Something caught my eye. Verse 1 said, *Now when Ezra had prayed, and when he had confessed, weeping and casting himself down before the house of God, there assembled unto him out of Israel a very great congregation of men and women and children: for the people wept very sore.*

My mind began processing as I studied the verse. *Why would these people gather around one man? What was so special about Ezra that these people were drawn to him?*

As I thought about what could have possibly been so different about *Ezra*, I remembered something I had just read back in Chapter seven. I flipped back a scanned until I found verse 10, *For Ezra had prepared his heart to seek the law of the Lord, and to do it, and to teach in Israel statutes and judgments.* That was it! Ezra had prepared himself to be used of God.

But how do I do that? I want You to use me, Abba, but I'm not Ezra! I'm not going to be able to change a nation, but I do what You to be able to use me right here, right where I am. Where on earth do I start?

I read *Ezra* 7:10 again. This time through, three words stuck out to me: seek, do, and teach. God started talking.

Three easy steps for you to follow, Nel. Seek to know my Word. Do that which you already know you're supposed to be doing. And then teach the truth to others.

That scared me. *I'm really not good speaking in front of people, Lord.*

I never said you have to be in front of people to teach. Look around you, Nel. Who is in your life that you would have the opportunity to teach about Me?

I remembered the conversation God and I had had about Tam. Then I remembered Amanda. God was giving me opportunities to share Him with others even before I realized that was what He wanted me to do. *God, You're so amazing! But I need your help. I can do the whole seeking Your Law thing. Doing it might be a challenge — You know how stubborn I am. Teaching it to others? God, I don't even know how that's gonna go. I need wisdom. Lots and lots of wisdom.*

I'll give you the wisdom you need in the moment that you need it. Don't worry about that part. Just trust me.

Tam started stirring in her bedroom. I heard her alarm go off and her groan as she reached to turn it off. She sounded crabby.

Lord, help me today?

Tam left the apartment by 9:00 Saturday morning without saying very much to me. She'd opted out of sitting on the patio that morning and had even declined a cup of coffee or orange juice. I couldn't tell what was wrong, but I knew something was up.

Left alone, which was unusual for me on a Saturday morning, I cranked up my new Hillsong CD and began tidying the apartment. By 11:30 I was starting to get hungry. I looked in the fridge. Tam hadn't done the grocery shopping yesterday like she'd promised.

What's going on with her?

Just then I heard a knock on the door. *Who on earth?* I wondered as I made my way to the door. I remembered to use the peep hole this time. Standing on my doorstep was Nic Spaulding.

I glanced down and realized I was wearing a grubby t-shirt and my cut off sweatpants had bleach stains on them. I was barefoot. At my height, without makeup and wearing casual clothes, I looked like I was fourteen.

Oh great. I thought. *Why does he always show up when I look like trash?!*

He knocked again.

I have to answer. It's not like he'll think I'm not home, my car's right there! I peeked outside again. He was still standing there with something behind his back. *Well. Here goes…*

I opened the door. "Hey, Nic."

"Hi!" Nic flashed me a smile. He didn't seem to notice what I looked like.

I ran my fingers through my hair. "What's up?"

"Oh! Um. Nothing. Not much." He was fumbling for words. "What are you up to?"

"Just cleaning up. Hence my appearance." I laughed nervously. *What's gotten into me?*

"What are you talking about? You look great!"

"Oh…" I didn't know how to respond.

An awkward silence hung between us now. Nic was shifting nervously from one foot to the other.

"Oh, hey!" he pulled a bag from behind his back. "I ordered lunch from Chile's and realized I ordered too much. Thought you might like to share?"

I'd love to! How did you know I'm starving?

"I don't know, Nic. The house really isn't ready for company, and I-"

"I'm not really company, am I?" he smiled. "I don't mind what your house looks like. I know you're cleaning but everyone's gotta eat. What do you say?"

I hesitated briefly. *Maybe if he sees my house a wreck he'll realize it would never work between us?*

"Okay. Sure, I guess." I opened the door wider. "Come on in."

Nic stepped through the door and surveyed the living room with a grin. Clean laundry was piled on the end of the couch, waiting to be folded. Figaro was tangled in a towel on the floor. "Looks like home!" he chuckled. "Which way's the kitchen? Or do you wanna eat out here?"

"Let's go to the kitchen. Follow me. Kind of ironic for me to tell you that, "I said with a laugh. I led the way through the doorway to the kitchen and asked, "Would you like some coffee? I was just getting ready to make a fresh pot."

"I'd love some! What's life without God and coffee, right?"

I froze with my back to him. *What on earth?! God, are you playing tricks on me?* My heart was beating fast and hard. How could two guys say the exact same thing, be so completely different from each other, but both seem to be so perfect for me at the same time? *Help me focus on You, God, and not let Nic or even Lance get to me.*

I started the coffee pot and turned to find the food laid out on the table. Nic had ordered the Southwest Eggrolls, nachos, and a Paradise Pie to go.

A man after my own heart! Lord, help me!

He had ordered exactly what I ordered every time I went to Chile's! Of course I always had a friend with me, I could never eat all that food by myself.

He looked up and found me looking at the table. He smiled. "This is what I always get, but I can never finish it all by myself." He grinned uncertainly. "Is it okay?"

"Okay? Yeah! It looks great!"

"Good!" he breathed a sigh of relief.

I grabbed two cups and poured us coffee. As I sat at the table Nic asked, "Do you mind if I pray real quick before we eat?"

Do I mind?! I would love it if you prayed before we eat! "Sure, you can pray."

We bowed our heads.

"Dear, Father, I thank you for the day you've given us to share. Thanks for letting us spend a little time together right now over this great meal. Help us not say or do anything that would embarrass or shame you, God. Please bless this food now and our fellowship. In Your name, amen."

Nic's prayer was more relaxed than when he prayed in church. I could sense that he had a deep personal relationship with God. At almost every turn, Nic Spaulding was surprising me – almost as much as Lance was surprising me at every turn.

What's going on, Lord? Am I really that horrid a judge of character?

Nic and I had an enjoyable lunch filled with small talk and getting to know each other. He really was a nice guy if you could get past that initial impression that he thinks it's all about him. I found myself completely relaxed and even laughing at his stories of all the mishaps of his first few months in ministry. By the time he left it was nearly two o'clock.

Just as Nic pulled out of the parking lot, Tamara came speeding in. She parked in a hurry and came storming into the apartment.

"I can't believe it! How can he *do* this to me? He can't honestly expect me to just pick up and move all the way across the country for his stupid career! What about me?! What about *my* career?!"

"Whoa! What's going on, Tam?"

"How can he be this selfish?! I don't understand!" She broke down in tears and ran into her bedroom, slamming the door.

Lord, can this be one of those moments You suddenly give me wisdom? Please?

CHAPTER 14

It was obvious to me what was wrong. Donel had moved up quickly in the ranks with the law firm Stockard and Associates after graduating from the McGeorge School of Law in Sacramento. The firm which specialized in patent law was based in San Francisco with a satellite office in Sacramento. Tamara had mentioned last week that Mr. Stockard had shared some good news with Donel about opening an office in the Big Apple. I remembered her lamenting about how she would die if Donel was asked to move to New York.

I put on a fresh pot of coffee, went to my room grabbed my Bible, and stretched out on the living room floor. "It's just You and me," I said as I opened His Word. *How can I comfort Tam in her obvious state of distress? What can I say?*

I got up off the floor and poured a cup of coffee. I walked around in a circle sipping my coffee. I was nervous. I felt a lot of pressure. The talk God had with me last Wednesday weighed heavier than ever on me now.

I'm not through Nel. Your roommate Tamara... she's watching you. I know you understand what I'm saying Nel. Tamara has a desire to know me, but she doesn't KNOW know me yet. That's where you come in. You're my ambassador.

I remembered His words with such clarity. He was depending on me. I was His *ambassador*, right here, right now. I knelt on the floor and opened His Word to *Proverbs*. I began reading at chapter 1 and verse 1. As I read, I prayed silently asking my Lord, my Protector, my Shepherd to guide me, to lead me, to provide me with whatever would bring her comfort. I read through chapter 1, then chapter 2. Nothing.

"Please Lord, give me something, a sign, a word, a thought," I said softly. I turned the page at the same time Tam's door opened. A drop of perspiration fell from my forehead and splattered on the page. I looked at the single highlighted verse on the page where the perspiration had begun to soak in:

Proverbs 3:5 Trust in the LORD with all thine heart; and lean not unto thine own understanding.

As I stood up and walked towards Tam, I thought, *Lord I am trusting You.* I wrapped my arms around her and held her. She was sobbing and I held her tighter. I held her and waited.

Lord, I am trusting You. Give me words to comfort her.

And as I waited on the Lord to give me something to say, Tam stopped crying.

Wow! And I thought I was trusting You, but I apparently was still depending on my own ability to comfort her with words.

Tam took my hand and led me over to the couch. As I followed behind her I looked up and mouthed the words *I get it.*

We sat down facing each other. Tam said, "Do you know what Donel did?"

"Well, I can imagine. Does it have something to do with his company opening an office in New York?"

"How did you know?" she said looking a little put off.

"You told me last week!"

"Oh. That's right, I did, didn't I?"

"So?" I was confident that I had figured out what was going on, but wanted to give Tam a chance to tell me. To let it all out.

"Well, Mr. Stockard told Donel that he would make Donel an associate if he would move to New York and work out of that office."

"Well, what's so bad about that?" I inquired.

"He said *yes* without ever asking me! I see that leaves me with three choices. I can go with him, I can stay here, or…"

I interrupted her. "Let me guess the third. You could kill him."

"Oh Nel, you crack me up. No that would be a fourth option," she laughed loudly.

"Well than, what would be the third?"

"I could just die," she said as she began wailing.

I wrapped my arms around her once again and held her tightly. "There's really only one choice actually."

Almost immediately she stopped crying and sat back and looked at me. "And what's that?"

"Trust in the Lord!"

The next morning Tam was up and had made coffee. As I sat on the patio sipping my coffee Tam went on and on about wanting to be more like me.

"No you don't. You don't want to be like *me* Tam."

"Oh yes I do. Nel, I have been watching you, and when I am around you, my life is so different. I don't have the pressures that I have when I am around Donel and his friends. Did you know that I have to watch my mouth whenever I have been away from you for a while. I'm always afraid I'll slip and use a *bad* word."

"No, I guess I didn't know that."

"Well, it's true. And Donel and his friends tell the crudest jokes, and they expect me to laugh at them."

"Wow, I didn't realize."

"So, last night I did a lot of praying Nel. You told me to trust the Lord, and that's what I am doing, and Donel can go to New York without me."

"Are you sure that's what you want to do?"

"Doesn't matter what I want to do. It's what God wants me to do. Now go get ready so we won't be late for church."

I went into my room, but before I got dressed I got on my knees beside my bed like I did as a little girl. I folded my hands and closed my eyes and with my heart humbled said, "Dear Lord, forgive me for my lack of trust in You, and my inability to see opportunities You provide to serve others and share your Word. Renew my faith in You and give me the courage to declare your Word to others. In His precious name, Amen."

I got dressed and walked out to the living room.

"Tam. I'm ready," I called out.

"In here," her voice came from the kitchen.

As I entered the kitchen, Tam looked up briefly from my Bible. "This is a *great* book!"

I smiled and said, "Is Donel picking us up?"

"No, he's on his way to San Francisco to meet with all the big wigs this afternoon. It's just you and me roomie. Wanna drive?

"Sure."

We piled into my Focus and headed to Straight Paths. We were greeted by Lance in the foyer. "Where's Donel?" he asked as he gave Tam a hug.

"Oh, he's history." She smiled, then turned and walked into the sanctuary stopping and saying hello to congregants on her way to sit close to the front.

Lance looked at me dumbfounded.

I looked at him, turned my palms up, and shrugged.

Lance followed me to where Tam was sitting. I stopped and said hello to Jim and Sandi. I could tell they were still trying to figure out my relationship, if there was any, with Lance. Matter of fact, *I* was still trying to figure that out!

The song leader opened with a contemporary song *How Great Is Our God*. At the end of the chorus without missing a beat, he led the congregation into *How Great Thou Art*. I felt the Holy Spirit alive inside me as I worshiped. I was sitting between Tamara and Lance and their two voices gelled nicely. I had never heard Tam sing out. I stole a glance at her. Her eyes were closed and she smiled broadly as she sang praises. I looked up and mouthed the words. *Thanks Lord. How great You are!*

The song service continued for nearly a half hour and I was ready to hear God's Word preached.

When Nic got up to preach, he surveyed the crowd, and with a look of great concern, said, "I am so ashamed." He paced back and forth on the stage, and once again he said, "I am so ashamed." The congregation sat in silence waiting for the shoe to drop. I could see Nic was overwhelmed by his emotions as tears began to run down his cheek. He said for a third time in a much softer voice, almost a whisper, "I am so ashamed, because I have missed opportunities to preach the gospel and tell this community of the one and only Truth!" His voice reached a crescendo.

"Yes Brothers and Sisters in Christ. I came here today prepared to preach one thing, and when I walked through the door and went to the altar, I said 'Lord, I know what I want to preach today, but is it what you want?' I said 'Lord, you tell me to trust in You and to lean not on my own understanding. Here I am Lord. Use me.'"

Everyone that had been there Wednesday night knew that the Lord was really starting to use Nic. The congregation had lost members over the years. Nic had been Pastor for about six months, and the core group had been praying that the congregation be a force for the Lord in the community.

"And you know what He said to me?" Nic looked in my direction, then across the aisle. Then he lifted his Bible with his outstretched arm and said, "He told me to tell you that *He giveth power to the faint, and to them that have no might He increaseth strength.* Isaiah 40:29."

He paused momentarily, then continued, "He told me to tell you to trust in Him, Jehovah, the God of Abraham and Isaac. He told me to tell you that if you trust in Him completely, He will deliver you in *every* situation just like He delivered the Israelites out of the hands of Pharaoh. That He will deliver you just like He delivered Daniel from the den of lions, and just like He delivered Shadrach, Meshach, and Abednego out of the fiery furnace."

Nic had walked down from the stage and stood right in front of the front row. He began to weep. "I know there are those of you that have put your trust in Him completely, and you have given me your testimony, and it is powerful. We need a fire in our belly to go out and share the Gospel of the one and only true God. We need to speak boldly. We need to, in the words of a young Christian blogger 'go public,' because as 1 Peter 2:9 says, … *ye are a chosen generation, a royal priesthood, an holy nation, a peculiar people; that ye should show forth the praises of him who hath called you out of darkness into his marvellous light.* In order to do this though you must *Trust in the LORD with all thine heart; and lean not unto thine own understanding.* Proverbs 3:5."

He padded his way back up onto the stage and turned around. "As your Pastor, I ask you to join me in asking the Lord to use us, use the members of this church in a mighty way. Ask Him to have his way with you."

The song leader stood and as he made his way to the pulpit he began singing,
Have thine own way, Lord! Have thine own way!
Thou art the potter, I am the clay.
Mold me and make me after thy will,
while I am waiting, yielded and still.

As we sang Nic continued speaking. "If you are burdened, cast all your cares on Him. Let Him have His way with you. Don't fight it. You can pray where you are or you can come to the altar."

I closed my eyes and continued singing. When I opened my eyes, I saw Tamara at the altar. She was surrounded by Sandi and some of the other ladies. They were all praying with her. I glanced at Lance. He looked at me and took my hand in his. I didn't resist. For some odd reason it felt right.

Monday morning I woke up smiling and feeling good about life and my renewal of life in Christ. I went to the kitchen to make a pot of coffee and enjoy some quiet time with my heavenly Father. Tamara was in *my* place reading *my* bible, and sipping coffee.. She looked up and gave me one of her big cheesy smiles. "Did I tell you this is a *great* book!"

"Yes, I believe you did," I said as I poured coffee into my smiley face mug. I sat down across from Tam.

"You know what else, Nel?"

"No, tell me Tam."

"I sat in my room and talked to Him, and He is like a friend that listens without interrupting. And it's amazing the way He makes me feel!"

Wow! God, you truly are amazing!

Tam and I sat and chatted and she told me all that God had revealed to her since Donel had made his choice to move to New York. I enjoyed listening to her talk about our amazing God, something we hadn't really shared previously, and before I knew it, the time was 8:50. *Yikes!* I had to be at work in ten minutes!

I scurried around my room, pulling on my skirt and slipping into a pair of sandals. I buttoned my blouse and looked in the mirror to check my hair. "Oh my!" I grabbed a hair tie and pulled my hair into a tight ponytail. *This'll have to do. My luck this will be a very busy Monday.*

I ran into the office at 9:12. Sandi was fielding phone calls and Jim was scrambling around the office like a chicken with his head cut off. He stopped momentarily and said, "You're late Nel. Did you forget this is Lee's vacation week?"

"I'm sorry Jim. Tamara, my roommate and I were talking about how God is working in our lives and how we feel so at home at *Straight Paths*."

Jim's harsh look softened, and he said, "Well get busy. Don't forget you're taking tomorrow off."

We were so busy, I worked through lunch and past five o'clock fueled only by coffee. I felt jittery and weak as I walked out the door. I debated for a moment whether to stop and pick up something to eat on the way home, but decided against it. I pulled up in front of the apartment and the smell of homemade spaghetti was drifting from one of the four apartments in our building. The windows were open in each apartment, and I would've bet the heavenly scent was coming from Mrs. Bellevue's apartment. I opened our door and my olfactory senses detected smells of garlic and basil and oregano drifting from the kitchen. Tam peeked through the kitchen door, and said dinner's almost ready.

I ran to the bedroom, kicked off my shoes, and rushed to the kitchen. Tam was stirring the spaghetti sauce and singing *Open the Eyes to My Heart Lord*. I glanced in the garbage can to spot if she was using *Classico* sauce or the cheaper *Ragu*. There was no evidence of store bought sauce. I picked up a spoon and got a taste of the sauce from the pan. "You made this?" I paused, "from scratch?"

"Yea. Is it that bad?"

"No! It tastes amazing," I said as I spooned up more sauce.

"Well, I just threw together one of grandma's recipes. It was easy. Besides I love to cook."

"I didn't know," I said grabbing a plate and helping myself.

I lifted my fork to my mouth. I was hungry and this smelled good. Tam grabbed my wrist and said, "We need to pray first. Will you pray Nel?"

Oh Lord. You keep reminding me that Tam is watching me and I keep forgetting!

"Of course."

After we finished eating we talked briefly about my upcoming lunch date with Brian. I was exhausted from work and told Tam I was turning in for the night. As I reached to open my bedroom door, I turned to Tam and asked, "Any good advice you can give me for tomorrow?"

"Absolutely!"

"Let's hear it."

"Trust God!"

The next morning Amanda arrived to pick me up at 8:30. I had called her Sunday afternoon and asked if she would like to go early and have lunch in the city with an old friend of mine.

I was waiting for her outside and hopped in her black Durango when she stopped. She was wearing blue jean cut offs that showed her atrophied legs. Her deep dark tan highlighted with little blonde hairs masked the lack of tone and muscle in her legs. Her upper body, on the other hand was solid and her red sleeveless shirt revealed her muscular shoulders and arms strengthened by her daily routines.

"Good morning!" she said vibrantly.

"Hey Amanda. How are you?"

"I'm great! Isn't this California weather fantastic? Such as beautiful day!"

"That it is!"

"By the way Nel. Where's your bikini?"

"Ha ha, very funny," I said examining myself. I was wearing a calf length jean skirt and a button up paisley blouse. "Do we have time to stop for a mocha?" I queried.

"For sure."

I loved her bubbly smile.

Amanda headed through the Starbucks' drive-thru and ordered a coconut mocha frappacino.

"Um, that sounds good," I said.

"Want one?"

"No, I'll have a quad, grande, non-fat, no-whip, caramel macchiato."

"Holy, moly… If, I had that much caffeine, we wouldn't be driving to the bay area, we'd be flyin!"

As she pulled up to the window, Lance appeared, holding our drinks. "How are my two favorite ladies?"

I felt my face flush, and I looked down as I fished around in my purse. I pulled out a ten and handed it to Amanda, but before she could take it, Lance said, "No way Jose, these are on the house."

"Thanks big brother," Amanda said as she took the beverages from Lance. He was grinning from ear to ear.

As Amanda passed my mocha to me, I said, "Thanks." My face still felt warm as I looked over at Lance and smiled. He looked at me and my eyes became fixed on his. He flashed me a smile and said, "Trust me, the pleasure is all mine!"

I felt my pulse increase, and despite the fact that I was sitting, my knees were weak.

The car behind us honked, and Amanda said, "We gotta run. See ya Lance."

Without taking his eyes off me, Lance said, "Later sis. See you later Nelia?"

As Amanda pulled away from the window, I turned my head and continued to gaze at Lance, drawn by his eyes and smile like a paperclip is drawn to a strong magnet.

We drove for about an hour just listening to the CD player. Amanda was only four years younger than me but her music made me feel like there was a generation between us. I asked her if we could stop at Dixon. I really had to potty. When we got back on the freeway she turned off the music and said, "So Lance tells me you go to church where he goes."

"That's right. I never see you there Amanda. Why don't you go?"

"Yeah. Well, I am not into all that *God* stuff. It's just something made up by men."

"Why do you think that?" I was genuinely concerned.

"Ask any professor or someone that has spent their life gaining knowledge if there is a God, and they will tell you that men have worshiped gods in one form or another since the beginning of man."

"And you *believe* that?"

"Of course. I mean science can explain how the universe came about over a billions of years and how living things evolved. It all makes perfect sense. Besides, if there was a God, why would he allow me to live most of my life in a wheelchair?"

What? Lord help me. Is she crazy?

"Amanda...."

"Yes Nel? Does that bother you?"

"I just don't understand how you can feel that way. After all, I believe that you are *alive* because there is a God!"

"You sound just like Lance. You live believing in this fairytale and that's all fine and dandy. But you cannot prove that God exists."

I had gotten into discussions with others that felt like Amanda and I made a fool of myself. I thought about Nic's Sunday morning message and *Proverbs* 3:5 *Trust in the LORD with all thine heart; and lean not unto thine own understanding.* "Use me Lord," I prayed silently.

I looked at the dash of the car and all the controls and instruments and I said, "Have you ever taken this car in for service?"

"Of course."

"Why do you get it serviced?"

"Because if I don't, it'll break down or wear out early. Why do you ask?"

"Would you say it is a complex machine?"

"Well yeah. What's your point?"

"Would you agree that the body is much more complex with all it's different organs and cell types and enzymes, and that as long as you add the proper fuel, it pretty much repairs itself and keeps on going?"

"I guess. I know the heart is amazing. It pumps the equivalent of millions of gallons of blood through your body in a lifetime."

I looked at her and smiled. "I don't believe that happened over eons and eons."

We sat in silence for several miles. I could tell Amanda was processing what I said. Finally she spoke.

"Hmmm. You do make a strong case for a creator."

I called Brian and told him we were passing by Berkley. He was at Fisherman's Wharf and had a table at the Bubba Gump Shrimp restaurant. Traffic was bad as usual and parking was even worse, but we happened to find a handicap spot a block away. I walked into the restaurant and spotted Brian. His hair was longer than I remembered. He gave me a hug and looked beyond me for my friend.

"What are you looking for Brian?"

"Your friend. Did he come?"

"Yes *she* came. Brian meet Amanda. Amanda meet Brian."

Brian appeared uncomfortable for the first few minutes as if he had never been around someone with a disability, but after we ordered and Amanda shared some of her life story he seemed very much at ease. In fact, Brian appeared smitten with Amanda. Even though I should've been thankful his attention was drawn off me, I felt a little put off.

We had only a half hour. Amanda told Brian she couldn't afford to be late for therapy. "They torture me if I'm late."

We all laughed at Amanda's joke. As we got up to leave Brian said, "Can I push you to your car?"

"Sure, you're the first guy that's ever offered to push me to my car. Most guys I know just want to push me off a cliff," she laughed.

Amanda's therapy lasted for two hours. On the ride back to Jackson, we talked a little about Brian. Amanda said despite their age difference she was attracted to him, and then she apologized for giving Brian her phone number.

"I didn't even know," I said. "Listen. You did me a favor!"

I then guided the conversation in another direction; I drilled Amanda about Lance. Finally, she got tired of my questions and said, "Nel. There are just some things you're going to have to find out for yourself." She turned on the radio and I fell asleep. When we got to my apartment, it was late.

"Thanks for coming with me Nel, and thanks for the chat. You certainly have raised more questions in my mind. I would love to talk more about this."

"Sure thing. Just let me know when."

I didn't feel like going to work Wednesday morning, but knew I had to. Tam was gone when I got up. I wanted to go to Starbucks. I wanted a mocha. No, actually, I wanted to see Lance. I opted to have my coffee at home. It felt good to have some time alone to seek God. I opened my Bible to a familiar passage. Romans 12:2 *And be not conformed to this world: but be ye transformed by the renewing of your mind, that ye may prove what [is] that good, and acceptable, and perfect, will of God.*

I looked up with my eyes wide open and said softly, "Lord, You have opened my eyes. Transform me today, renew me as I seek to do Your will. In Jesus name. Amen."

I flitted around the office like a butterfly, gracefully completing my tasks, and answering the phone with joy in my voice. The day was over before I knew it.

On the way home, I stopped by the coffee shop. I went inside hoping to catch Lance and tell him how the talk with Amanda went. I looked around, but no Lance. When I got to the counter, I asked the guy taking orders if Lance was in the back.

"Oh, are you Nel, the girl he is so in love with?"

I was taken aback. "I'm Nel."

Well, sorry Nel, but Lance didn't show up today.

Hmmm. That's interesting.

Tamara arrived home from work and I was sitting on the couch playing with Figaro. It was 6:30. "Why aren't you ready?"

"Ready for what?"

"Church silly! Church starts in half an hour, and I don't want to be late!"

Wow. What a difference.

On the ride over to church, I told Tam about Nic not showing up for work.

"It's probably nothing to worry about Nel. He probably just needed a break."

"Yea. Maybe you're right. I *hope* you're right!"

Nic was greeting people when we arrived. He chatted briefly with Tam and I and as we started to walk away, he grasped Tamara's hand with both of his and said, "I am praying for you and Nel. Praying that the Lord is working on your hearts and minds, to use you; so watch for those new doors to open up."

When we sat down Tamara leaned over to me and whispered, "I know the Lord is using you Nel. I've seen how people react to you. Do you think He can use me like He uses you?"

I was perplexed. *Lord where has she seen me used. What is she talking about?*

I took Tamara's hand in mine and squeezed it. "Oh Tamara. Believe me, He will use you. Like Nic said, be ready."

Nic challenged the congregation again to be bold and trust in the Lord. He ended his lesson saying we must live like the Apostle Paul citing Galatians 2:20 *I am crucified with Christ: nevertheless I live; yet not I, but Christ liveth in me: and the life which I now live in the flesh I live by the faith of the Son of God, who loved me, and gave himself for me.*

He had an altar call and moved to the back of the sanctuary to allow people time to pray.

Tamara and I were the last to exit the sanctuary. Nic asked us how we were doing and then said, "Nel would you excuse us for a minute, I would like to speak to Tamara alone. "

.I walked to the car.

Tam had a confused look on her face when she got in the car.

"What's wrong? What did Nic want to talk to you about? Care to share?"

"He asked me out."

CHAPTER 15

I sat in stunned silence. It wasn't that I was expecting or even hoping that Nic would ask me out, but I was blindsided by the news that he'd asked Tamara. I didn't even know they knew each other!

"What?!" I looked at Tam, shocked. She looked just as surprised as I felt. "That's really……. random! I didn't even know you guys knew each other!"

"Well I've seen him here at church…. And a couple of times around town."

"And you haven't told me about this because….." The silence hung between us for what seemed an eternity.

Tam looked at me pleadingly, "I knew you were kind of interested in him and that Sandi's been trying to set the two of you hooked up! And I was dating Donel at the time and I knew he'd kill me if he somehow found out that Nic bought my coffee a couple of mornings-"

"He *what?!?!*"

"He bought my coffee, but it wasn't anything weird or anything! He just so happened to be behind me in line and recognized me from church and we got chatting and it just happened! I didn't even flirt in the least bit with him, Nel, I mean…. He's a *pastor*!"

"Oh, Tam."

"I'm sorry." It was as if she were literally melting into the seat. She buried her face in her hands. "I'll tell him no. That's the only option. He can't possibly want to go out with *me*. He's a *pastor*!"

Thursday morning rolled around early, bringing with it a heavy heart and some mild confusion. I decided not even my favorite coffee from home would help me this morning and headed to Starbucks for the strong stuff. Lance was MIA once again. I was starting to get worried.

I hope nothing happened with Amanda!

I purchased my quad shot caramel macchiato and headed to work. It was a quiet day with only two couples coming in to book a vacation together to Honduras. Sandi helped them make their arrangements and everyone else stayed busy in their offices, quietly shuffling papers and surfing the web for the best destinations to suggest to potential clients. Jim sent me home right after lunch.

"No need for all of us to be sitting here waiting for the coffee to brew. Just go home, Nel." He turned to go back in his office and stopped, "You know what? Go ahead and take tomorrow off too. Enjoy your weekend."

I couldn't remember the last time Jim had given me a day off 'just because'. But I wasn't about to complain! I thanked him and headed out the door.

What to do with my free time? I knew if I went back to the apartment and stayed that I would be bored out of my mind. Tam would be at work and Figaro does nothing but sleep in the afternoon. I didn't even feel like watching a movie or driving to the lake. My phone alerted me that I had a new message. It was from Nic.

I need u ASAP. Meet me @ the church. If u r working just tell Jim I need u. It's important.

I wondered what could have him in such a bind that he needed *me*. I hurried to the apartment and changed out of my business clothes into a knee-length jean skirt and my *Alice in Wonderland* t-shirt. I slipped my flip-flops on and ran out the door. I had no clue what he needed but I wanted to be comfortable.

As I pulled into the church parking lot I noticed there were only two other cars there. Nic's black Volt was parked in the spot marked "Pastor's Parking" and the other car parked just a few spaces away from Nic's made my heart stop. I quickly parked my car and ran inside with a prayer running through my heart and my breath caught in my throat.

I stood outside Nic's office door, trying to hear what was being said. They were speaking in low tones and I couldn't make out what was being said through the closed door.

Should I knock? Do I even want to know what's going on in there? Lord, remember that wisdom we were talking about the other day? Yeah. Well. I could use some right now!

The door swung open and I found myself face to face with Nic. Brian stood just behind him. I could tell he'd been crying.

"Oh! There you are, Nel!" I could tell I had startled Nic. "Brian said you two were old friends; we've just been getting to know one another."

There was an awkward pause where we all stood staring at each other. I wasn't sure I wanted to know what the two of them had been talking about.

Brian broke the silence. "Hey, Nel." He said quietly.

"Hello." I was unsure where to go from there. My curiosity kicked in. "What are you doing here, Brian?"

I guess I spoke rather sharply because Nic's brow creased and I could tell he was studying me. But at that time I didn't care. I crossed my arms, waiting for Brian to explain.

Finally, Brian took a deep breath and told me, "I've been under a lot of…. stress…. lately, Nel. A lot has been happening. My sister, Taylor, was in a car accident last month and she's still in hospital, pretty beat up. I lost my job, which is why I'm out here for the interview; I screwed up bad this time, Nel." He hung his head. I could see tears rolling down his face.

Nic took that chance to slip away and give us time to talk alone. I was grateful that I didn't have to wonder what he was thinking while trying to understand what Brian was telling me.

Brian gathered himself and began speaking again. "I lied, cheated, and manipulated my way to the top, babe, and everyone finally saw through my charade. I've been so lost these past few months. I was dating a girl and we were pretty serious, but when all this happened she left me. My parents," he laughed bitterly, "you know my dad. He won't even let me in the house. Says he's ashamed to call me his son. Claims he'll never speak to me again unless I get my life straightened out." He broke down again weeping.

I wasn't sure what to do or say. I wanted to reach out and hold him, wipe away his tears, but I was not entirely sure this wasn't just another of his stunts to gain control of my emotions. I didn't want Brian back in my life and I was beginning to wonder if I ought not warn Lance for Amanda's sake. In the middle of my quandary, Brian began speaking once again.

"I've been searching, Nel. Searching for purpose, for a goal, for something..." I could tell he was struggling for the right words. "I've been searching for something like you have."

I stopped breathing.

"I haven't been able to get you out of my mind, Nel. Not for emotional or physical reasons or anything like that, but for something deeper. I remember when we were together that you would go to church sometimes and you always prayed right before you ate. We both claimed to be Christians and we were doing the same things as far as God was concerned but you were different." He paused and looked at me.

I was frozen. I was looking at Brian but, for the first time, I was seeing a vulnerability and completely open and honest side that I had never before seen in him. It was like I was seeing a completely different man.

"Brian, I... I don't know what to say."

"You don't have to say anything. I don't expect you to forgive me for everything I put you through. I don't deserve your forgiveness. But of all the people I need to talk to in order to make things right, you were the first one I wanted to tell." He took a deep breath. "Nel, I got saved today."

Brian's eyes were filled with tears again but this time they were accompanied by a huge smile spreading across his face. He stood there in front of me with his hands in his pockets, weeping and laughing all at the same time.

"But... I... you..." No coherent thoughts were coming to my mind. All sorts of thoughts were there, but none of them would get organized into a complete thought and find their way out my mouth.

Brian reached for my hand, "I wanted to talk to you about it on Tuesday, but then you brought Amanda and I felt awkward bringing anything up so I just didn't say anything."

"But..." Finally, a thought came to me. My original question. "But why are you *here*?!"

He chuckled. "Well, I was actually coming to find you to see if we could talk and I got a bit turned around. I ended up here. I saw the car in the parking lot and decided I'd come in. What better place to find answers about God than at a church, right?"

"Right."

I still just stood there, my hand in Brian's hands. Of all the possibilities and scenarios that had played through my mind between the time that I saw Brian's car in the parking lot and the moment Nic opened his office door, this had not even crossed my mind. I had assumed the worst. I had planned what to say in defense of my character to Nic and even all the things pent up inside of me these past three years that I wanted to say to Brian. All of those words were gone now. I was speechless.

"C'mon." Brian headed for the door, dragging me along behind him. "Let's go get a coffee and we can talk all about this there. I think you're in shock or something."

We walked into Starbucks and standing behind the counter was Lance. He looked up and saw me. A smile spread across his face and he said, "Well, hello there, my lovely lady-" He noticed Brian's arm around my shoulders. "And who's this?" His smile had vanished as quickly as it had appeared.

"Uh… This is… well…"

Brian jumped in. Extending his hand across the counter he introduced himself. "My name is Brian. Brian Gentry. Nel and I go way back," he gave my shoulders a squeeze, "don't we, babe."

I could feel the tension in the room and I saw Lance's jaw tighten.

"I see." Lance replied. There was a tense moment of silence before he spoke again. "What can I get you two?"

"I'd like a venti vanilla latte please," Brian ordered. He looked down at me, "You still get the quad upside-down caramel macchiato, right babe?"

I nodded.

"Yeah, I know what she gets." Lance snapped.

Brian pulled out his wallet to pay and I wandered to a table in the corner. I was so confused about what Brian was telling me that I couldn't even muster enough willpower to show Lance I wasn't interested in Brian. *This just keeps getting better. Why did Lance have to decide to show up to work now of all the times he could have showed back up?! What must he think of me?*

We drank our coffee and Brian told me all that had been happening in his life and what had brought him to the point that he realized his need of salvation. Everything he said had the ring of truth in sincerity. I didn't doubt for one second that what he was telling me was true. He really was a changed man.

By the time we finally finished, we'd been in Starbucks for nearly two hours. We stood up to head to the car and I glanced behind the counter. Lance wouldn't even look at me.

"Brian, can you wait outside for me?"

"Sure, Nel! Everything okay?"

"Yeah. I just need to talk to someone real quick."

Brian studied my face.

"I promise! Everything's fine."

"Okay. If you say so." He headed out to the car and I made my way to the counter.

Lance pretended not to see me. He was wiping down counters and banging around syrup bottles. I had never seen him so upset before. *Do I even want to try to talk to him right now? Lord, I need You!*

"Are you gonna talk to me or just stand there, staring?" He grumbled.

"I'll talk to you if you'll at least look at me."

Lance scrubbed at the counter a bit more before finally turning to look at me. He crossed his arms and leaned up against the counter. When I saw the look on his face I almost wished he *wouldn't* look at me. It might have been easier to talk to his back.

I gulped. "What's going on, Lance?"

"Are you *serious*?!" he laughed harshly. "You're asking *me* what's going on?"

"Yeah! I am!"

"Don't you think I should be asking you the same question?"

"Perhaps." I crossed my arms, matching his defiant pose. "But I asked first."

Lance shook his head and looked down at his feet. I could tell he was upset at me but he had absolutely no reason to be! It frustrated me that he would automatically assume anything about Brian and me. *Lance, of all people, should know me better than that.*

I could see Lance's jaw flexing. His eyes flashed. *Why is he so upset with me? It was one coffee! It's not like I'm marrying Brian for Pete's sake!*

"If you don't talk to me, Lance, I'm walking out. Now's your chance."

He took a deep breath and let it all out. "I've just needed some time to think. That's all. I took some time off."

"You took time off church too? I didn't see you on Wednesday."

"I left town for a bit, alright? I can do that. It's not against the law for a guy to go on vacation for a few days."

I studied his face. He was hiding something, I was sure of it.

"I talked." He said. "Your turn. Who's the guy?"

By this time, I was so frustrated with Lance that my stubborn side kicked in. *He thinks he can keep secrets? Fine. So can I!*

I spun and headed out the door, calling over my shoulder, "He's my ex!"

CHAPTER 16

My life was in total chaos, I thought as I rushed to my car. My mind was, simply put, in a state of confusion. I asked myself, *Why would Lance be at all interested in me? I am certainly nothing like his type. Why could something seem so right and so wrong at the same time? And why isn't Nic more interested in me? I am exactly his type. After all, the Chambers women are bred to be pastors' wives. And what's up with Brian? After three years he suddenly is back in my life, and I want to believe him. I want to trust him. But I don't know. And then there's Tam. I blew it with her last night. I need to make things right with her. Lord help me!*

I stopped at a four way stop and checked my rearview mirror to see if Brian was behind me. Over coffee, the two of us had decided we would go to my apartment and talk about things, very important things – like where he was going to stay, what he was going to do, how he was going to make things right with his family and friends – and, about *us! Yikes!*

While I was stopped, I had an epiphany. I remembered when dad taught me to drive, and even way before that when I would cross the street with mom, they would always said: "Stop, look, and listen." *That's what you're telling me to do. Right God?*

"You're saying to stop and focus. Look for danger. Wait, wait, wait… I know that scripture! Um. I got it! *First Peter* five verse eight. *Be sober, be vigilant; because your adversary, the devil, as a roaring lion, walketh about, seeking who he may devour.* And then listen. Listen for your directions."

I turned to see Brian standing alongside my car; I rolled the window down.

"Are you talking to yourself? Are you okay?" He said with a puzzled look.

"Yea. I mean no! No I mean yes, I'm fine."

"Are you sure?"

"Well, no. I think I may be coming down with something. Let's get to my apartment."

Tam wasn't home when I arrived. I didn't know how she would react to him being at the apartment considering Tam and I hadn't seen or spoken to each other since last night. I decided to text her.

Hi Tam when will u b home?

She fired back an immediate response. *I didn't think u wanted me 2 b around me!*

Brians here. Wanted to give u a heads up

Oic well ill b there whn I get ther

Kind of cold I felt, but then again, *didn't I deserve it?*

I told Brian to make himself comfortable; then I said, "Be right back. I need to take care of some things."

He looked bewildered and asked again, "Are you sure you're okay?"

"No, I am not Brian, but what can you do? You are part of the problem, alright?"

Gulp. *Oops. Oh Lord! How can I look and listen if I don't stop first?*

Brian hung his head and headed for the door. I could see tears streaming down his cheeks. "I'll just leave," he choked out between sobs.

"Oh Brian! I am so sorry. I didn't mean it like that," I said as I reached for his hand. "I don't know what I'm doing or what I am saying. Will you forgive me? Please?"

His head was still hanging as he turned to face me; he couldn't bring himself to look me in the eyes. "Of course I'll forgive you, after all that I've…"

"Shhhh," I said as I placed my finger on his lips. I kissed him on his forehead and I could see the corners of his mouth turn up ever so slightly.

"Please Brian. Just sit tight out here in the living room while I go take care of some personal business." I hesitated momentarily and finished my thought, "with God."

Figaro was laying on the bed stretched out with his head resting on my Bible. "Sorry to bother you old buddy, but mommy needs her Bible." My feline companion opened his eyes and stretched as if to say *Don't bother me now.*

I opened God's Word to the book of *Second Peter. I know that scripture about being vigilant and sober is here somewhere in this epistle.* I had a lapse of memory perhaps or more likely it was divine intervention. I began scanning chapter two and stopped my finger on verse 9 and read it with a whisper, *"The Lord knoweth how to deliver the godly out of temptations…" That's a good one Lord. Thank you, but why can't I find that scripture about the devil seeking to devour? I just recited it in the car with book, chapter, and verse number. It's on the tip of my tongue.*

Not being able to recall that scripture had me frazzled and then it came to me. All I had to do was stop, look, and listen. It was in *First Peter* chapter 5 verse 8. I quickly turned back a few pages to find it while keeping my finger on *2 Peter 2:9. Oh Lord my God,* I thought. *You are so clever. Wow! Like two pieces of a puzzle fitting together 2 Peter 2:9 seems to follow 1 Peter 5:8 perfectly.*

I read the verses out loud, "Be sober, be vigilant; because your adversary, the devil, as a roaring lion, walketh about, seeking who he may devour. The Lord knoweth how to deliver the godly out of temptations…"

Stop, look, and listen. "So is that what you are trying to tell me Lord?" I asked out loud.

I heard the doorbell ring. I knew it couldn't be Tamara; she had a key.

There was a gentle knock on my door, and I heard Brian ask, "Would you like me to get the door?"

I said "Sure," figuring what else could go wrong.

I heard Lance and Brian talking in the living room. I didn't know if I should exit my room or stay put and wonder what was transpiring. I couldn't imagine that Lance had come to apologize. But then again, there were a lot of things I could not imagine about Lance.

My feelings where Lance was concerned were very much like a ride on the *Medusa* at Six Flags Animal Kingdom. I remember the first time Tam and I went there together just after we became roommates two summers ago. I was so uncertain about going on that thrill ride, Tam had to coax me to stay in line. Then once I was locked in the seat, I grabbed Tam's hand and I felt a lump in my throat. Then climbing that first hill, I was terrified, and the ride down was even scarier I closed my eyes as we did the loopty loo, and the sensations that ran through my body were both exhillerating and electrifying. When I got off the ride I turned to Tam and said, "I never felt so alive." That's kind of how it felt with Lance.

I reached for the door. A documentary on *fear* that had aired on the Discovery Channel came to mind. I remembered how biologists had observed that mammals, in particular, released certain enzymes when they sensed danger; hence the phrase "smelled of fear." *If that is true of humans,* I thought, *I must wreak fear!*

I began to recite the *23rd Psalm*. *"The LORD is my shepherd; I shall not want. He maketh me to lie down in green pastures: he leadeth me beside the still waters. He restoreth my soul: he leadeth me in the paths of righteousness for his name's sake."*

I opened the door, closed my eyes, and continued as I walked into the living room, taking the liberty to change some of the words. "Yea, though I walk through *my own living room where Lance and Brian happen to be*, I will fear no evil: for thou art with me; thy rod and thy staff they comfort me."

I stopped when I could hear the two of them breathing.

"Are you okay?" They said in unison.

"Yea. Sure. Why wouldn't I be?" I said nervously.

Lance spoke up. "Well for starters, you're walking around with your eyes closed reciting what sounded like a unique version of Psalm 23." He looked at me and shrugged his shoulders with his palms up, and of course, he flashed me that endearing smile.

Oh my soul. He was upset with me not two hours ago. Now look at him, I thought. *How can I be upset with him?* I looked up and whispered, "Lord, please intervene. Now, please."

"Please forgive me Nelia for being such a jerk," Lance pleaded.

How do I respond Lord? Shouldn't I be the one seeking forgiveness?

Brian looked at the two of us and said, "I'm going to step outside for some air." With that, he sidestepped between the two of us and hurried towards the door.

As he reached for the door knob, I heard the lock click from the outside. The door opened and Tam glanced at me, and then to Lance and pointing with both hands to her bedroom door said, "Just going to my room."

Lance suggested we go into the kitchen to avoid further distractions or interruptions, and so I led the way, filled my smiley face mug with yesterday's coffee, and popped it in the microwave. Words could not describe the odor that filled the room from the day old coffee being reheated. I turned to Lance and said, "Want a cup?"

He said, "I know I deserve to die, but please, not *that* way." He grabbed his throat with both hands for emphasis.

I chuckled.

Lance's face then took on a serious look, and he said, "Would you like to tell me about this Brian guy? He didn't want to say much to me."

"Only if you'll tell me why you went AWOL on me."

"Okay deal."

"You first," we both chimed simultaneously.

"Okay. I'll go first. Would you repeat the question please?" Lance said.

I looked straight into his eyes and with my best Raymond Burr impression I queried, "Where were *you* on the night of June 17th?"

Our eyes locked, and he reached out, put his hands on my waist, and pulled me towards him. He needed no strength to pull me because I was drawn to him like a moth to a flame. He held me within an inch of his body, looked down at me, and said, "Nelia. I don't want to hear about Brian, I want to know where I stand with you."

Lance caught me as I fainted.

I was only out for a minute or two. When I opened my eyes, I was lying on the couch, and Tam was holding my hand. A tear rolled down my cheek as I apologized to Tam for acting like a teenager. She said she was as much to blame as I was for our little *tiff*.

Lance was sitting on an ottoman patiently waiting to resume his conversation with me when the door opened and Brian popped his head in. "Knock, knock. Can I come back in?"

There were no objections so he strode in and took a seat. "So Nel. Where am I sleeping tonight?" Brian inquired.

"What?" Lance quipped as he came off the ottoman.

"Brian, would you excuse us for a minute? Now!" I said as I sat up and pointed at the door.

He quickly exited.

I looked at Tam.

"No way am I leaving Nel. This, I gotta hear!" She laughed and looked at Lance, then back at me.

"What in the name of Jehosophat is going on? Is he, your *ex*, staying *here* with *you*? Lance asked.

"We hadn't discussed that yet."

"When were you *going* to discuss it?

"Yea, I'd like to know that myself," Tamara chuckled.

"Very funny Tam!" I glanced at Tam with my teeth clenched. I looked back at Lance. "What suggestions do you have?"

"He's welcome to stay at my house. There are three empty bedrooms."

"Well that's mighty generous of you Lance, but I don't think that would be a good idea."

"Why not? Are you afraid he might give up some of your little old secrets?"

"No, it's a bad idea because he and Amanda were flirting with each other last Tuesday."

"My little sister? We definitely have a predicament on our hands!"

CHAPTER 17

Brian knocked before opening the door this time.

"Can I come in now, babe? Is it safe?"

I saw Lance's jaw tighten. *I'm going to have to talk to him about actually using my name. Especially around other people, namely Lance!*

"Yeah," I answered. "It's safe." We had been talking and left him out there for nearly thirty minutes.

Brian made his way into the apartment and plopped down on the couch beside me. He was dressed in expensive khakis and a bright blue polo with the collar popped. I could feel Lance studying the two of us. *He's probably wondering what on earth I ever saw in Brian. He seems so shallow now that I look at him compared to Lance, or even Nic. Lord, what did I see in him?*

I could hear God speaking to my heart, saying, *Judge not, Nelia.*

"Snap out of it, Nel." Lance was staring at me with a slight grin on his face.

"What?"

"You were zoning out, babe." Brian draped his arm around my shoulders and smiled.

"My name is Nel, Brian, *not* babe." I smiled sweetly up at him.

Tam glanced around awkwardly. "Um. I think I'm gonna make some coffee. Anybody want some? Okay then!" She didn't wait for an answer before heading into the kitchen.

Brian waited a moment before speaking. "I know it's not your name, silly, but I just thought… ya know…" He glanced toward Lance who now stood with his arms crossed and his back to the door.

"I know what? Just say it, Brian."

"Well…" he glanced toward Lance again. Lance raised his eyebrows, sending a silent challenge.

"Speak, Brian. You can say whatever you want in front of Lance."

"Oh, really? He knows about us, does he?"

"Brian. Stop."

I could see the defiance coming back to Brian's eyes and a little part of me felt justified for having doubted his 'conversion' earlier that day. *I knew it! He's just faking all of it. Well, it's not going to work this time!*

Almost as quickly as it appeared, the look in Brian's eye passed and he stood up from the couch, walked to the chair, and sat down.

"I was just thinking that maybe we could try this again." He glanced at Lance and lowered his voice. "But do it right this time."

I took a deep breath and glanced at Lance. "Can we not do this now? Just…. not right now."

"Okay."

Lance still stood with his arms crossed and staring at Brian as if he were sizing him up and trying to figure him out. I was doing the same but more in my heart than in my head. *Lord, you know the rush of emotions that always come when Brian is involved in my life in any way. Him coming here – now – has got me all tied up! I don't know which way to turn or what to do, God! Please help all of this to work out for Your glory. Oh…. Can I have some wisdom while You're at it? Please?!*

Brian and Lance stayed for dinner. Tam whipped up a quick 'breakfast-for-dinner' of scrambled eggs, French toast, and bacon. My favorite. It was exactly what I needed to calm me down and help me focus on the task at hand. *Thank you, Lord, for an amazing and understanding roommate!*

Lance had informed me that Amanda was staying with a friend in the city for a couple of weeks. Because his work schedule had been changed he wanted her to have someone who could take her to therapy and be with her at night. It just worked better having her stay with a friend than always trying to figure out a way to have someone go with her all the time. Lance decided Brian did not need to know that Amanda was his sister. At least, not yet. I was unsure about the arrangement, not knowing exactly how I felt having Lance and Brian alone under the same roof for an indefinite amount of time. But what other choice did I have? None.

Friday morning found Tam and I curled up on either end of the couch, sipping our coffee and listening to the heavy rain outside. We'd both woken up early and spent time reading the Bible. Tam seemed quieter than usual but I was lost in my own thoughts of Brian and Lance and wondering how their first night alone in the same house had gone. I wanted to text Brian but I wasn't entirely sure I wanted to know what was happening at the house.

Lance sat at his kitchen table remembering the events of last evening. Never before had he felt so protective of any woman, unless you counted his sister. I had a way of bringing out the protective side in him. He felt slightly bad about the way he had acted when he saw me and Brian together in Starbucks but seeing us together made him realize how much he cared for me. He'd never experienced such a sharp feeling of jealousy as he had felt that afternoon.

God, he prayed. *I don't understand all of these emotions but I know You do. I like Nel a lot but I don't want to lead her on in any way if there's nothing for us beyond friendship. I know I don't deserve a girl like Nel, but I can't ignore the way she makes me feel. I just want to glorify You, God. That's all.*

Lance heard Brian coming down the stairs and prayed one last time for patience and wisdom before Brian came sauntering into the kitchen. He was wearing designer jeans and a red Hollister t-shirt. He looked like he had just walked off the pages of a magazine. *Is that really what Nel is attracted to? I didn't imagine her being that shallow. But, maybe? Have I just been looking at her good looks and totally missed who she really is?* Lance didn't think that was the case but Brian interrupted his thoughts.

"So. How's it going?"

"Great." Lance sipped his coffee and just stared at Brian.

Brian stood with his hands on his hips and looking around as if waiting for Lance to wait on him. When Lance didn't offer anything further, Brian asked, "Mind if I have some coffee?"

"Sure. Go for it. Cups are in the cupboard right above the pot."

"Thanks."

Brian went about getting a cup of coffee while Lance observed him from behind. *What could Nel have possibly seen in him? He's so….. preppy. He doesn't seem like her type at all.* Lance thought for a moment. *But what if he is her type? Where does that leave me? Out in the cold, that's where. She'll never go for a guy like me if he's the type she's into! What was I thinking?*

Brian turned and asked if Lance would mind if he joined him at the table.

"Sure." Lance replied, wondering what they could possibly talk about. He said a quick prayer for grace and patience. "So, Brian, what do you do for a living?"

Brian hesitated. "I've actually been an investment banker for the past five years. But I'm getting out of that now and looking into other options."

"Cool."

There was a long pause as the two men tried to think of something else to talk about. Lance took a deep breath. "So…. Where are you from?"

Brian laughed slightly, "Nel really hasn't told you anything about me, has she."

"Nope." Lance shook his head. *I'm not sure I really want to know anything about you either, but for Nel's sake I'm trying to be friendly.*

"Well," Brian set his coffee cup down and leaned his forearms on the table. "I grew up in D.C. My dad worked in government for years and always wanted me to follow in his footsteps. That didn't happen," he said with a hint of bitterness. "I went to college with Nelia in Boston and got into investment banking then. My dad wasn't too happy with me, but, whatever. And now here I am."

Lance thought for a moment. "So, you just did the investment banking thing to make your dad ticked off?"

"Partly, perhaps. But it doesn't matter. He's a drunk; has been for years. Rich drunks are the worst. They make their way through life, paying people off to cover their tracks and expect everyone to look the other way. But then the little guys like me come along and try to do the same thing and those same people condemn us and kick us out of their society." Brian hung his head. "You wouldn't believe me if I told you all the stuff my dad has gotten away with just because he's rich. It makes me sick."

This guy may not be all bad. But he's still totally wrong for Nel!

"But if he's rich, doesn't that make you rich?"

"Not really. He disowned me when I didn't go into government work and now with everything that's happened over the past few years he doesn't want anything to do with me." Brian hung his head. "Why am I telling you all this?" he laughed. "I should be asking your intentions toward Nel!"

Lance hesitated. "We're friends."

"But *you* want more?"

"I don't know what I want right now. But I do know that I have to leave for work or I'll be late." Lance stood from the table.

"Oh, that's right. You're a barista."

Lance could sense a mocking tone in Brian's voice but he wasn't sure if it was just his pride making it seem like there was something there or if there really was. He chose to let it slide. *What could Nel possibly see in a guy like Brian?!*

Brian sat sipping his coffee at the kitchen table after Lance left for work. *What could Nel possibly see in a guy like Lance?*

All thoughts of Amanda seemed to be gone from Brian's head by Friday afternoon. He had sent six texts to me by the time noon rolled around and he showed up at the travel agency wanting to take me to lunch.

"I can't go with you, Brian. I was planning to work through lunch and just go home early."

"Nah. You need to take a break!" He grabbed my hands and tried pulling me from my chair. Just then, Jim opened his office door and stood staring at the two of us. We froze.

"What's going on here? Who is this, Nel?"

I pulled my hands free of Brian's grasp and stood up. "This is Brian." I answered. "An old friend from college."

Brian's brow creased. Jim looked him up and down once. "Need to get a haircut, Brian. You look like Italian mafia or something with your hair all slicked back like that."

Nelia stifled a laugh.

"Better that than a politician." Brian spat back.

Jim looked at Brian thoughtfully for a moment before turning to me. "I'm not sure what you see in these guys with shaggy hair, Nel. First that guy from church and now him? You need a clean-cut guy like the Preacher."

Brian didn't even try to hide his laughter at that. "A *preacher*? Nel? Yeah right! That'll never happen!"

Jim and I glared at him.

"I don't know who you think you are, creep," Jim scowled. "But I think you need to leave my agency. Now."

The tone in Jim's voice left no room for argument. Brian headed toward the door.

"I'll text you, Nel." He said as he pushed the door open. "Have a nice day, sir." He nodded his head toward Jim.

The door shut behind him and I stood in stunned silence. *What in the world just happened?*

"Listen, Nel." Jim tapped my shoulder. I turned to him. "I don't know what has gotten into you but you need to focus. What's the best thing for you? One of those two bums or the preacher? I don't know who that guy thinks he is, but I think Nic is a great guy and the two of you are perfect for each other! What's the holdup?"

I wasn't sure how to respond. I didn't know if I should tell him that Nic had asked Tamara to go out with him or if I should just leave it alone. It wasn't really my place to tell him that was it? Nic should be the one to tell Jim and Sandi to lay off. Right?

"I'm happy single, Jim. They're all just friends." I cringed. Was that really true? I wasn't technically dating any of them!

Jim studied me for a moment. "Well, okay then. I'm gonna drop it, girly. But you need to make up your mind." He handed me the file he'd been working on and went back into his office, shutting the door behind him.

Ugh. God, can I please just move to Russia or Mongolia or something? This is just too frustrating to think about! Nothing in my life is going the way I thought it would or even remotely close to the way I want it to go. Whatever happened to You giving me the desires of my heart? Not saying I really know what they are right now but You're God, You should know what they are and just handle all the details for me. Right?

I waited for God to answer. My cell phone rang.

"Hello?"

"Hey, Nel." It was Lance. "Can I stop by the office for a sec?"

"Ummmm…. I'm really not sure that's a good idea right now. I think I'm gonna run back to the apartment and grab a sandwich. Wanna just meet me there?"

"Sure! I'll see you in ten!"

The call ended and I sat there quietly. *That wasn't your answer was it, God?*

CHAPTER 18

On the ride home I tried to imagine what Lance wanted to talk to me about. When I pulled up in front of the apartment two familiar cars were there. Tam's and Nic's. This took my mind off of the varied thoughts of what Lance wanted to talk to me about.

I hesitated at the door, but then I thought *Nic's a pastor and Tam doesn't seem to be interested in him. After all, I remember what she had told me: 'He can't possibly want to go out with me. He's a pastor!'* I took my apartment key from my purse, inserted it into the lock, then paused again. *So what could he be doing here – with Tam, alone?* I stood there, mentally anguished, key in the door, thinking about what was going on inside. I had completely forgotten about Lance, *and* Brian. For some odd reason, I felt a surge of jealousy over Nic showing an interest in Tam.

Nic is my type and I am his type, I thought. *He is not Tam's type and because, he is a pastor, Tam is most definitely not his type.*

Satan had tricked me again!

What are you thinking Nel? God was chastising me, and He reminded me of a scripture. My dad had me recite Ephesians 6:12 on a regular basis, because he knew that the mind is a battlefield and a favorite place for Satan to frolic and play.

For we wrestle not against flesh and blood, but against principalities, against powers, against the rulers of the darkness of this world, against spiritual wickedness in high places.

I was so concerned with what might be transpiring in the apartment, I didn't hear the approaching footsteps. As I turned the key a hand fell to my shoulder and I jumped and spun around in mid air. Lance quickly assumed a jujitsu pose and just as quick cracked a big smile.

"Nelia. What on earth is going on with you? You look like you just saw a ghost! Well except for the fact that your color just went from a pasty white to a crimson glow with matching splotches on your arms. Very cute!" He was laughing out loud now. He didn't even catch his breath. "You don't have to try so hard to win my heart Nelia. It's yours for the taking, and I'll wait as long as it takes for you to reach out and grab it."

How do I respond to that? No one has ever pursued me like Lance except Brian, and he had ulterior motives. Lance seems to be genuine, and I like that he goes to church regularly.

I smiled it Lance. *But what about Brian and oh Lord, what about Nic?*

Lance reached for my hand and said, "Well?"

I took his hand and shook it and said, "We'll see. Only time will tell."

Lance and I entered the apartment. Nic and Tam were sitting beside each other on the couch. Tam's hands were in her lap; Nic had one hand on Tam's shoulder, the other on Tam's hands. They were both praying inaudibly, and were so deeply immersed, they didn't even realize we had walked in.

On Lance's cue, I followed him to the loveseat and sat down beside him. He took my hands in his and began to talk to God softly.

'Lord. Thank you for this wonderful day, for the numerous blessings that you have granted me, especially Lord for that gift of Salvation…. "

A prayerful thought quickly sailed through my head. *Thanks Lord for that little revelation. Makes my life easier and harder at the same time.*

Lance continued, "I am honored to be able to come to you and to caste all my cares on you. Please Lord forgive me for not being Christ like with Brian, and forgive me in the many areas where I fail you…"

This provoked another thought, although not a prayerful one: *What in the world happened this morning?*

I opened my eyes briefly to steal a glance at Lance. Tears were in his eyes.

"…and precious Lord, Creator of all the Heavens and the Earth, I have one big burden on my heart, a request that in my little human thinking mind seems all important to me. Lord, You know I have prayed diligently and earnestly for you to provide a woman for me, a real god-fearing woman, and I have asked for the discernment to recognize when you have put that woman in my path. I believe you have answered that prayer. Now Lord, can you soften her heart towards me and show her that I am right for her. In Jesus precious and holy name, Amen."

I looked at Lance. His eyes met mine and I said, "Amen."

Nic and Tamara had finished praying and had assumed a more relaxed posture on the couch.

"So what brings the two of you here," Nic asked.

I looked at Lance for direction, and he appeared to either not know what to say or just not want to answer.

I remembered the time Lance rescued me at Starbuck's and I decided to return the favor.

"I was coming home to eat and offered to fix Lance lunch."

"Did you stop at Starbuck's and see him?" Nic pressed for more.

Oh my soul! I can't believe I just distorted the truth and to a pastor of all people.

Lance decided it best to jump in. "Actually, I needed to talk Nelia, so I called her and she offered to meet me here."

"Well don't let us stop you. After all, we're all Christians aren't we?" Nic said.

I must've glared at Tam, because she stood up, took Nic by the hand and said, "Let's you and I go try that new sushi place."

Nic looked puzzled as he let Tam lead him out of the apartment.

I was overcome with a rush of jealousy as I watched them leave.

I was beginning to feel like I was suffering from what my dad called wilderness mentality. Had I become like the Israelites who after God's amazing deliverance out of the hands of Pharaoh, were still not happy? After they were freed from slavery to the Egyptians they complained and questioned why God would bring them into the wilderness to die rather than allow them to die in slavery. But God didn't desert the children of Israel and He had given me assurance that He would not desert me as I recalled Isaiah 41:10 *Don't be afraid, for I am with you. Do not be dismayed, for I am your God. I will strengthen you. I will help you. I will uphold you with my victorious right hand.*

"What was it you wanted to talk to me about Lance?" I was almost afraid to ask.

Lance looked at his watch and said, "I don't have enough time now, I have to get back to work."

"When would you like to get together again?" I asked hesitantly.

"How about tomorrow? I work the morning shift, off at two. How about I drive you to San Francisco, we go by and visit Amanda and then I take you to dinner?"

"You mean like on a date?" I giggled feeling at ease once again.

"Yea. Like a real date. Just you and me Nelia."

I love the way he says my name.

He was at the door and I was still sitting on the loveseat.

He walked back towards me, and I got up to meet him. He stood in front of me; my heart was racing. A part of me wanted to turn and run, but another part of me wanted to fall into Lance's arms. He leaned over and kissed me gently on the forehead. I felt my face flush.

He smiled and said "See ya."

I was speechless.

When I returned to work, Jim and Sandi were conferring in Jim's office. They both glanced at me as I walked over to the coffee pot. Sandi came out of the office and summoned me to Jim's office.

Jim said, "Take a seat Nel."

I sat, tugged on my skirt slightly, and put my hands in my lap interlacing my fingers.

"I'm sorry about the interuption earlier today with Brian," I said.

"Nel, we just want you to be okay," Jim said.

"There are so many creeps and nuts in this world Nel, and we know that Pastor Nic is a Godly man," said Sandi.

"I know I told you I would drop the subject, but Sandi and I talked and we insist that you come for lunch this Sunday. Nic will be there and we will be sure the two of you have ample time alone."

I began, "But.."

"No buts," they both said in harmony.

"Now get back to work," Jim said.

I got up and returned to my desk feeling defeated.

Thoughts of Lance permeated my mind all afternoon. Occasionally a thought of Nic would infiltrate my brain and sometimes the realization that Brian had managed to find his way back into my life would creep up on me. I had poured myself a final cup of coffee, and that's when it hit me! I needed to have a chat with God. I returned to my desk, and began silently praying, hoping for no interruptions.

God, you are all knowing, all powerful, omnipotent, omnipresent, and you love me so much, you sent your only son to die in my stead. I know you don't need my help Lord, but if I could make some suggestions for the man that I believe would be perfect for me... he would have heart like Lance, be laid back and funny like Lance. And Lord, you design us Chambers' women to be pastors' wives, you know, you put it in our DNA; so the perfect man for me would have a couple of Nic's qualities — handsome and a pastor of course, and last Lord, whatever it is that Brian has that makes me feel the way I do when I am around him, please throw that into the mix.

I had closed my eyes and apparently my lips were moving. Sandi was walking past me when she looked at me, paused, did a double-take, and then said, "Nel? Are you okay? Are you talking to yourself?"

Caught off guard, I felt my face flush as I snapped, "No. I wasn't talking to myself!"

"Well, then who pray tell were you talking to?" Sandi asked.

"Well I was um…"

"Something's really troubling you isn't it hun?"

"No. Well yes. I was actually praying."

"Having a little time with God? Why didn't you ask me to pray with you. I *love* to pray! What were you praying about?"

"Well, Sandi. It's kind of personal."

"Aw Nel, you know we are all family here. We want to bear your burdens with you," she said with a concerned look. "What can I pray for you sweety?"

"Well," I said, "I was actually asking for God to send me a good man."

"You know the Scriptures say, 'Ask and it shall be given you, seek and ye shall find,'" Sandi said in a motherly fashion.

I felt a tinge of conviction. "I wasn't actually asking God for a good man. It was more like I was telling Him what the perfect man for me would be."

Sandi gasped. "Oh my Lord Nelia. You shouldn't do that! Where is your faith?" She placed her hands on my shoulders and lifted me up from my chair, wrapped her arms around me and held me tight. "Nel," she whispered in my ear, "Open your eyes. Pastor Nic is single and he is a godly man!"

On the ride home, I began to think, *Maybe Sandi and Jim are right. Maybe Nic is the man that God has designed for me.*

I had no plans for the night except watching reruns of Law and Order and playing with Figaro. I was tired of Panda Express so I decided to swing by Chili's and pick up a taco salad. As I pulled into the parking lot, I saw Tam's car and Nic's car parked conveniently together. A lump formed in my throat.

Lord, are you trying to say Nic is unavailable? What's going on?

I didn't want to see them together in there. *After all,* I thought, *they had lunch together earlier, and now dinner. Pastor or no pastor, two single people, one of them being my gorgeous roommate Tamara — well, that spelled romance!*

I whipped my car around and sped out of the parking lot headed for Panda Express. I was, tired, hungry, hurt, and terribly confused. I parked my car, paused for a minute, and thought, *I'll just grab some food, go home, eat, and instead of watching TV, I would read my Bible.*

I reached over to grab my purse from the passenger seat and Brian jumped in the car.

"Hey babe! Have you missed me? I've really missed you. I was just going in to buy dinner for you and me and bring it over. You still like that honey walnut shrimp, right?"

"Brian. You cannot just start popping into my life like this. It's over!" As soon as those words came out of my mouth, for some unknown reason, I regretted it.

CHAPTER 19

Brian slowly nodded and looked away. "Okay then." He said as he opened the car door. "I'm sorry."

Way to go, Nel. What a loser I am! I thought.

"No, Brian." I touched his arm. "I'm sorry. I didn't mean that. I'm just really frustrated and confused right now. I would love it if you'd bring food to the apartment."

He looked at me for a long moment before responding. "Okay. But only if you promise me we'll try to figure *us* out."

"Of course." I sighed. "We need to do that. I'll meet you at the apartment." I said as I shoved him out the door.

I wiped the kitchen table down as I waited for Brian to arrive with our dinner. It seemed as if God were telling me to take the time alone I had been given to talk some things out with Him. I found myself babbling about all of my troubles.

God, I just don't get it! How can Lance seem so perfect for me and yet so incredibly wrong at the same time? And what does Nic, a pastor, see in someone so shallow and conceited as Tam? Are you trying to show me that Nic isn't all people think he is? Is he hiding some deep secret sin and this is Your way of telling me he's not as perfect as he seems? And why on earth is Tam encouraging him? She knows there's no way it could ever work between them. She is SO not cut out to be a pastor's wife; I AM! Nic is practically everything I've always wanted in a guy. He's got the looks, the mannerisms, and the passions that I've always looked for in a life mate. Why can't he see that?!

And what's up with Brian? Why on earth did he have to come back now? Of all the times he could have possibly popped back into my life, why now? Just when I was confused enough with Lance and Nic, Brian has to show up and have the sob story of ruining his life and then having a 'glorious conversion' and now wanting to make things right with me! Why on earth now, God?

I heard a knock on the door and someone opened it.

"Hello?" It was Brian.

"In the kitchen!" I called.

Brian came in carrying the Panda Express bag and a drink tray holding two venti Starbucks cups.

"I thought we could both use the caffeine." He explained.

"Oh my soul, yes!" I reached for the cup marked as having four shots of espresso and inhaled the intoxicating aroma. *He remembers my drink? Why, God? Why does he have to be so sweet?* I took a sip of my quad shot, upside-down caramel macchiato and let the liquid linger on my taste buds. *You know what?* I thought. *I don't even care. Thank you, God, that he's here!*

"You okay, Nel?"

I opened my eyes. Brian stood there with a quirky, inquisitive look on his face.

"Yeah. Why wouldn't I be?"

"You look like you're hearing the angels sing or something." He laughed. "Where are the plates?" he asked as he started opening cupboards.

"To the left of the sink." I pointed to the cupboard. "Do you know how long it's been since I had one of these babies? A *long* time." I sighed as I deeply inhaled the heavenly aroma.

"Whaaaat?" he quipped. "You used to drink those things all the time!"

"Yeah, well… people change." *I don't want to tell him I'm watching my weight! How embarrassing!*

"People change, sure, but that's your drink, Nel. C'mon. Do they not make it right out here in Cali or what?"

"No, they make it just fine."

"Then what?" He chuckled.

"Nothing!"

"Are you trying to lose weight or something, Nel?" He stepped up beside me and looked closely at my face as I felt it slowly turning red. "You *are*!"

"You don't have to sound so snotty for having figured it out!" I punched his arm.

"What? No!" he laughed. "I just don't see why you're concerned about your weight; you look great!"

"I do *not* look great!"

"Yes, you do."

I stuck my tongue out.

"Oh, how mature of you, Nelia."

"Be quiet." I took another sip of my macchiato. "I'm just surprised you remembered my drink."

"Of course I remember your drink." He looked down at the table. "I remember a lot of things, Nel."

I was unsure how I should respond. *Is he for real, God? Is this all just a charade to lure me back into a relationship? It's not going to work! I won't let it happen!* Brian looked up at me and I could see remorse written all over his face. *Oh, heaven, help me.*

"I'm sorry, Nel."

I turned my back to him and pretended to be looking for something in the silverware drawer.

"What for?"

"You know what for."

When I didn't respond, Brian came over and laid his hand on my arm.

"We need to talk about this."

This was a different side of Brian than I had known before. He was gentle, not forceful. He sounded sincere enough but could I trust him?

"I said I'm sorry, Nel, and I mean it. I blew it. I was wrong, and I'm sorry."

I looked into his eyes. *Lord, I need Your wisdom right now. Can I trust him? And what if I do forgive him and then he wants to rush back into a relationship? I know that's not what You want for me! Right? This isn't Your way of telling me I need to be with Brian, is it? Ugh. I'm so confused!*

I took a deep breath. Nothing was coming to me.

"Let's eat! I'm famished." I declared as I turned away from Brian.

"Stop!" he sounded frustrated. Brian grabbed my shoulders and turned me to face him. "Just stop, Nel. I've asked your forgiveness and I want an answer. I'm not here to force you into something you don't want to say or do but I'm not going to stop until you give me an answer – *any* answer!"

Something was tugging at my heart. I wasn't sure if it was God or if it was simply due to Brian's persuasiveness.

"Any answer?"

"Any answer."

"Do you promise?"

"Of course."

"Do you *promise?*"

"Yes, Nel. I promise. No matter what your answer is, I'll drop it after tonight. I won't bring it up, I won't hold it over your head, and I won't be upset."

I hesitated. Brian could see the uncertainty on my face.

"You have my word, Nel – for whatever that's worth."

Brian's face betrayed nothing besides sincerity and deep regret.

What choice do I have? God, I could use a bit of Your wisdom right now!

I took another deep breath. "Of course I forgive you, Brian. But that doesn't mean I can just forget everything that happened between us."

"Of course not. I don't expect you to."

"And it definitely does *not* mean that I'm going to just jump right back into a relationship with you!"

"Well that's a given."

"I don't even think that it's wise for us to *consider* a relationship at this point, if ever."

"I agr... Wait. What?" Brian looked confused.

"I said that I'm not sure it's wise to even think about trying the whole relationship thing again."

"I heard you the first time. But what do you mean? Why are you saying that?"

"Well, because. You just accepted Christ and my life is confusing enough as it is without having to worry about how things will work out with us. I think it's wise for both of us to realize we can only be friends. You need to grow as a

Christian and I need to figure out what God's trying to teach me right now with all of my craziness. I'm sorry, Brian, but we can *only* be friends!"

Brian's face remained emotionless for a moment.

"You're serious?"

"Yes, Brian. I'm dead serious."

A smile slowly spread across his face. Suddenly, he laughed and pulled me into a tight embrace.

"Whoa! What in the world?! What's gotten into you, ya crazy?"

"I'm just so… so… *thrilled*!"

"You're *what*?!" I pushed him away and stood with my hands on my hips.

"I'm thrilled!" Brian laughed again. "Maybe relieved is a better word? I don't know. Anyway, I'm happy." He sat down and began serving himself pieces of mushroom chicken.

I couldn't think of anything intelligent to say. The only word that came to mind was, "What?!"

"No, I'm serious! I came to Jackson with every intention of wooing you and fully expected you to just fall right back into my arms, but then I talked to Nic before I found you and everything changed, Nel. I got saved and ever since then I've been so confused about us. My head keeps telling me we're right for each other and I have to have you but it just doesn't feel right and now here we are! You just said everything that I've been thinking and didn't know how to verbalize!" Brian froze and then looked at me. "Wait a sec. Nel! Do you think that was God preparing me to hear what you had to say? Do you think *God* was actually *talking* to *me*?"

I crossed my arms, "Okay. Who are you and what have you done with Brian?" I studied him carefully.

"Har har." He said sarcastically. "I'm serious, babe. Is that how He works?"

I found myself looking into the face of a man I had known for six years and it seemed I was seeing him for the first time. Brian Gentry was a changed man.

Saturday morning rolled around and I awoke with a smile on my face. *Two o'clock!* was all I could think. I wanted to tell Lance what had happened last night with Brian but I wasn't sure how to start the conversation.

Maybe I should practice conversation starters. No, that's dumb.

I got up and quickly showered before heading to the kitchen to make the coffee. I found Tam sitting quietly at the kitchen table with a Bible open in front of her. She was already dressed and ready for the day.

"Good morning!" I greeted her cheerfully.

"Hey."

Something was up. *Do I really want to know what's going on? I wonder if she and Nic had an argument or something. Not that they're dating or anything……. Are they? Hmmmm*

"Nel, I have a question."

"Oh! Okay?"

"So……" Tam was struggling trying to put her thoughts into words. "Okay. If a person is reading the Bible and going to church and all that stuff but still feels like something is…. missing, I guess you could say…. is something wrong with them? Do they just need to do more stuff to make them feel better? I mean, do they need to pray more or something?"

"What do you mean?"

"Never mind." She closed her Bible. "I need to go. I'll see you later."

She got up from the table and rushed out the door before I could say anything else.

Ummm Okay? Lord, I don't know what's going on there but, um…. Help?

 Lance showed up at 2:30 in Amanda's car.

"No clue why, but I feel like we should take her car." He shrugged.

"Fine by me!"

Lance and I rode the entire way to San Francisco without once thinking of Brian or Nic. He spent the trip asking questions about my family and growing up in northern Wisconsin. It was a pleasant ride and I was completely relaxed and unconcerned about all the uncertainty and confusion in my life. Being in that car with Lance seemed to wipe away all my anxiety.

We arrived at the house where Amanda had been staying and walked to the door. Lance knocked. We waited several moments but no one came to the door. Lance walked around the side of the house and looked in the back. He returned a few seconds later and said, There's a car in the alley; they *must* be here," as he reached to ring the doorbell.

We could hear someone running down the stairs. The front door swung open and we were greeted by a lady in her mid thirties with wiry blonde hair.

"Finally!" She huffed. "I thought you'd never get here. She's in the back bedroom. *Please* take her away!"

I was shocked. Lance took off towards the back of the house calling Amanda's name. The lady stood there staring at me with one hand on her hip.

"Is everything alright? Is Amanda okay?" I queried.

"Yeah, she's fine," the lady sneered. "As long as you consider burying her head in the sand and blindly following a dead man 'fine'." She stomped back up the stairs. I was even more confused now than when she'd first opened the door.

I waited on the front steps for Lance. He appeared from around the corner pushing Amanda's chair. She carried her small bag on her lap.

"Let's go." He said calmly. "Now."

Amanda had insisted on riding in the back seat. I could tell she was crying because I could hear her sniffling and her breath catching as she was trying not to make any noise. Lance wasn't saying anything and I decided to follow his lead. We were headed back to Jackson.

I glanced at Lance and saw in the corner of my eye that Amanda was clutching a book. I couldn't tell what it was but it looked old. The book was bound in what appeared to be brown leather and the edges looked faded from years of use.

That's not a Bible, is it?

We rode in silence the first forty-five minutes. Amanda broke the solitude.

"Nel?"

I jumped. "Yes?"

I knew Lance saw me jump; he was fighting off a chuckle – I could see the smile teasing the corners of his mouth. *So I scare easily. Big deal!* I mentally poked his arm and stuck my tongue out at him.

Amanda looked thoughtful. "Do you remember the conversation we had before? Not the one where you were picking my brain about my brother, but the other one. The one about God?"

I blushed. Lance wasn't even trying to hide his smile now.

"Yes, of course I remember, Amanda."

"Well…." She took a deep breath. "I believe."

"You believe?" I wasn't sure what she meant.

"I believe. I've been pushing it away for so long and trying so hard to *not* believe but I just can't get away from it!"

"I don't understand what you're talking about."

Amanda chuckled. "All of it, silly! I don't know why, but I packed my mom's Bible before I went to my friend's house. For whatever reason, I felt like I just had to have it with me. Well I started to read it the other day and it seemed like every page, every verse, was shouting the same thing to me over and over again. 'God is love! God is love! God is love!' I couldn't get away from it! I read the accounts of the crucifixion and realized all over just how much God loves me. And then I remembered the stories about the blind man and the crippled boy and Lazarus and how things happened to them so that God could get the glory. It made me realize that, no matter what happens in my life, whether good or seemingly bad, God has a purpose for it! Me being angry at Him and even being so foolish as to say that I don't believe He exists doesn't change the fact that I'm in a wheelchair. He put me here for a specific reason. Getting angry doesn't change His will for me, it just delays my understanding of why He's put me here. His will is for me to be right here, right now, just the way I am. I realize that now! Nel, if you hadn't said what you said I never would have come to this point! If it weren't for you I'd still be bitter and all shriveled up inside! Thank you so much!"

Amanda wasn't the only one in the car crying then. Lance reached over with his hand opened. I placed my hand in his and his fingers wrapped around mine tenderly. It felt right. I didn't know what to say.

"I tried witnessing to my friend, but she didn't want to hear it." Amanda explained. "She's been one of the ones encouraging me away from God and religion of any kind. She's so misguided and bitter."

"Is that why she wanted you gone?"

"Yes."

"I see." I wiped my eyes with the back of my free hand. "I'm so proud of you, Amanda. You coming to that realization on your own will strengthen you as a Christian even more than if I or your brother had just told it to you. God is going to use you in a great way to touch someone through your testimony."

"I hope so." She said sincerely. "I know if God can forgive me for the years that I've been questioning Him and even doubting His existence, He can show someone else just how awesome He is. Even without my testimony He can do that, but I hope He chooses to use me in some small way to teach someone about His love and forgiveness."

"He will, Amanda. He will."

We arrived back at Lance's house and got Amanda settled into her room. She decided to take a nap and Lance and I headed to the kitchen.

"I have an idea."

"Oh really?" Lance asked.

"Yes, really. Is that so surprising?"

"No, not at all!" he grinned.

"Uh huh. Well," I paused for effect. "What do you think about me just making us dinner here since we didn't get to go out?"

Lance looked surprised. "You cook?"

"Of course I cook! Why wouldn't I cook?"

"No, I just didn't know that you could!" Lance sounded pleased. "It's tough to find a woman of our generation who isn't so focused on a career that she doesn't learn how to cook and stuff."

"I learned how to cook when I was very young." I explained. "I remember watching my mom at the counter from the time I was little. She used to pull a chair over and let me stand on it so I could watch; I was too short to see otherwise."

"So, last week?" Lance chuckled.

"What?"

"You were too short to see. So that was last week, right?"

"Hey! That's not funny." I tried punching his arm but his hand caught mine before it made contact. He grabbed my other hand and spun me around until I was twisted in my own arms and couldn't get away. I was giggling in spite of the short joke.

My back was to Lance and his chin was rested in top of my head. We were quiet and still, comfortable enough in each other's presence that the silence didn't feel awkward.

Just then, Brian came walking through the kitchen door. I jumped so bad it made Lance bite his tongue.

"*AH*!" He howled. "Ooooohhhh. Man! Ouch."

"I'm *so* incredibly sorry, Lance! Oh my word. Are you okay?"

"Yeah, I'm fine." He actually laughed. "You really *do* scare easily, don't you."

I felt myself blushing.

Brian spoke. "I didn't interrupt anything, did I?"

"Not really." I sighed. "I was just getting ready to make some dinner for all of us."

"Oh ok."

Brian was hiding something behind his back and he looked as if he were wanting to say something but unsure of how to say it.

"Everything alright, man?" Lance asked him.

Wow. They seem chummy.

"Um. Yeah, I think so." Brian pulled a picture frame from behind his back and looked at it thoughtfully.

Brian turned the frame toward us. It was a picture from last Christmas of Amanda kissing Lance's cheek. It was her favorite picture of the two of them and she insisted on displaying it on the mantle in the living room. Lance and I realized at the same time that we hadn't told Brian that Amanda and Lance were brother and sister.

"Not trying to cause problems, but why is your friend kissing the guy who wants to be your boyfriend?"

Lance jumped in. "Dude, she's my sister!"

"Huh?"

His head bobbed up and down, "True story! Amanda is in fact my little sister."

"But why isn't she here? Where does she live? I've been here how long now and I haven't seen her once." Brian sounded confused and a tad desperate.

"She's here now." I explained. "She's been staying with a friend in San Francisco but Lance and I brought her home this afternoon."

"Can I see her?"

"No." Lance answered firmly. "She needs to get some rest. Why don't we just make sandwiches tonight for the three of us and you, little lady," he tweaked my chin. "can come over Monday night and make dinner for all of us."

"That would work too, I suppose," Lance said with a smile.

"That way I can get groceries. Just tell me what you want and I'll pick it up, okay?"

"Sure. No problem."

"Better yet!" Lance exclaimed. "Let's go shopping together tomorrow afternoon between services!"

I smiled. "That sounds like fun."

"It's a date!" Lance gave me a quick hug. "Okay, I need food."

By the time I got home Saturday night, I was exhausted. Lance, Brian, and I had eaten our sandwiches and then played game after game of Dutch Blitz. The two of them were both so competitive that they couldn't just let the other one win. I'd finally left at 10:15 and they were still playing.

Lord, I don't fully understand Your timing or Your plan but I do know You're doing something here. Thank you for the friends you've given me in Amanda, Tam, Lance, and even Brian and Nic. I know each of them has a definite purpose in my life, I just need to be patient and let You work it all out the way You want it to work out.

There was a knock on my bedroom door and Tam came in.

"Hey, you!" I said. "What's up?"

"I'm going to Hell, Nelia! I'm going to Hell!"

CHAPTER 20

Tamara fell on my bed grabbed a pillow and pushed her face down into the pillow muffling her cries for relief, understanding, comfort. "Lord, please help me Lord. I don't understand what's going on! Please help me God!"

I knew she was under conviction, but not knowing the circumstances surrounding the opening of her eyes – the realization of her need for something that she was missing, I wasn't sure what to say.

I quickly sought wisdom as I silently prayed, *Dear God, Lord of my life, I come to you now in this hour of immediate need for your wisdom and guidance. I am both honored and humbled by your using me as an instrument in Tam's life to help lead her to the foot of the cross, where she can lay down all her burdens and accept your gift of salvation. These things I ask in your precious and Holy Name. Amen.*

As I finished praying, a calm fell over me and I was at peace with the mission God had put me on, apparently from the day Tam and I first met.

Tam lifted her head out of the pillow and it was evident to me that God was working not only on Tamara, but He was bringing me to a place where I finally recognized what He meant when He said that He was all I needed.

I looked at Tamara, my beautiful, flirtatious, flamboyant, perfect in every sense of the word, woman. A woman that most men would consider themselves lucky if she even looked in their direction. But it was only at that moment, when she raised her head out that pillow, eyes swollen and puffy from crying, mascara running down her cheeks, her hair in a frazzle, that I recognized her as the way I felt and the way I looked before I met the Master.

Tears began to roll down my cheeks as I wrapped my arms around a woman who was perfect by the world's standard but terribly broken by God's standard. And for the two years Tam had known me, she had been watching me, a child of God, even with my imperfections, live very differently than her other friends.

We held each other close; I could feel her heart beating and our tears comingled on our cheeks as they were pressed together. I felt a sense of relief in her so I released my hold and sat back. She assumed her favorite yoga pose on the bed in front of me and after struggling to move into a similar pose, I folded both legs to one side. She reached out and took my hands and said, "Nel, if you only knew how envious I have been of you for the past several months."

I thought, *Yes Lord, I'm finally understanding!*

She continued, "If you only knew what a living hell my life has been, and now after spending time with Nic and studying the book that you were always reading, you know the Bible, I just realized that I am bound for Hell."

She choked a sob. "I had dinner with Nic the other night, and we talked about life after death. He told me that it was serious business and I should go home and read the Bible and he gave me specific scriptures…"

There was a long pause, and then I broke the silence. "Well, did you read the scriptures he gave you?"

"Well of course. I studied them, but there was something else he said that I think you should know."

She paused again, like she was searching for the right words to use, and I thought, *God, I know I need to be more patient, but is now the time for that?*

"Well? What did he say?"

Unknowingly I had raised my voice. Tamara jumped as if she were snapped out of a trance.

"Patience is a virtue," she said.

"Is that what *he* said?"

"No. No. He said I should talk to you about salvation. He said he sees Christ living in you. That you not only talk the talk, you walk the walk."

"He said all that about me?"

"Yep. And he said he would be happy to pray with me and talk with me more about what it's like to live my life for Christ, but he said, your testimony and your understanding of the challenges of a young woman living for Christ would be far superior to his."

"He really said all that?"

"What? Do you think I would lie to you about something this serious?" She said as she began to cry again. "I'm already going to hell. I don't want to make it worse."

I almost blew it, but God was there in the room that evening giving me guidance. I reached for my Bible with one hand and took Tam's hand with my other.

"Lord, I recognize that you have placed a heavy burden on my friend and roommate's heart so that she will come to truly know You. You have opened her eyes, her ears, and her mind to your Word. Now Lord as we open the Scriptures and study them together I pray that You will open her heart to your gift of salvation. In Jesus name. Amen."

By the time I said "amen," Tam had gone from sobbing to full blown crying. She choked the words out, "Nel. I don't want to die and go to hell. I am so scared. What is it that I have to do to be saved. To live for Christ like you do. Just tell me. I don't want to go to hell."

While I listened to Tam, I turned my Bible to Romans 3:23. When she paused I read the verse out loud, "For all have sinned and fall short of the glory of God."

I had held my thumb at Romans 6:23; I quickly flipped the pages and read, *"For the wages of sin is death, but the gift of God is eternal life in Christ Jesus our Lord."*

Tam seemed frustrated when she said, "I know all that Nel. I've been reading that stuff. I know I am a sinner and I'm bound for Hell. Tell me how to be saved!"

"Well, you have to admit you're a sinner."

"I know Nel! What else?"

"You must be willing to repent of your sins. In other words, turn away from a sinful life."

"I will. What else?"

"Believe that Jesus Christ died for you on the cross and was raised from the dead," I said as I quickly turned to Romans 10:9 and read, *"...if you confess with your mouth the Lord Jesus and believe in your heart that God has raised Him from the dead, you will be saved."*

"I do believe that will all of my heart! What else do I need to do?" She said as a mixture of emotions seemed to show on her face, relief, excitement, fear, joy.

"And finally," I said, "through prayer, you ask Jesus Christ to take control your life through the Holy Spirit. There is nothing I can do, nothing Nic can do. It's all between you and our Lord and Savior!"

Tam wrapped her arms around me and almost squeezed the breath out of me. "Nel? Can I borrow your Bible tonight. I've noticed that you have a lot of passages highlighted and underlined and I have been reading those, and they make a lot of sense to me."

"Sure. Take your time."

"Okay. Oh, and Nel?"

"Yes?"

"No offense, but I want to go to my room and spend some time with my Savior. Are you okay with that? I mean if I don't chat with you more tonight."

"Tam, I would be offended if you kept our Savior waiting any longer!" I said as I handed her my Bible and pushed her towards the door.

That night I praised God for opening my eyes to both my weaknesses and my strengths.

Sunday morning I was awakened by Tamara in the kitchen belting out *When the Roll is Called Up Yonder* at the top of her lungs. The aroma of fresh coffee filled the air. I sensed that she was coming towards my door as I crawled out of bed.

I headed towards the door anticipating her knock. But before I reached the door, she opened it, the only warning being the sound of her voice appearing closer.

It appeared as though the timing was perfect as the door opened she ended the chorus *When the roll is called up yonder I'll be there* with an emphasis on the *I'll*. She had a glow about her as she handed me my smiley face coffee mug filled with fresh brew. "Good morning roomie. Time to get up and at 'em. We don't want to be late for church."

I looked at the clock. "But it's only eight. Church doesn't start until ten thirty."

"Oh Nelia. I thought we would walk to church today and enjoy some of God's wonderful creation."

"But it's supposed to be mid 80's today."

"Oh. Come on. You keep sayin' how you want to lose those extra holiday pounds. This would be a good way to do it."

Her bubbly approach and smile were killing me.

"Can't we go to the gym instead?"

"Nel. When do you *ever* go to the gym? Besides, Lance will probably bring us home!"

Exercise, God's creation, Lance bringing us home. Who could argue with that?

"Okay Tamara. You win. But I'm wearing my flats!"

CHAPTER 21

The Sunday morning service found me nestled into the pew between Lance and Brian; it wasn't nearly as awkward as I thought it might be. Amanda was wheeled in beside Lance at the end of the pew and was wearing the biggest smile I had ever seen on her face. Tam was seated at the other end, to Brian's left, and was quietly humming *Jesus Loves Me*. Tam was sparkling from the inside out.

It felt right to be there at that moment. Surrounded by friends who were all seeking the same thing that I was seeking – to glorify God. I was filled with a peace I never knew existed. I suddenly realized God was giving me that sense of belonging I had been seeking. When I gave up trying to satisfy my own loneliness and trying to figure out who the perfect guy would be, God was able to give me not only one friend, but five. Each of us was so different from the others, but together, we were exactly what we all needed. Our individual weaknesses were strengthened by our new friends and all of us were growing in our relationships with God. I found myself getting antsy for the preaching to begin.

Nic stepped up to the pulpit and announced his text. I said a quick prayer to God.

Abba, You're so amazing! I never imagined that day when I decided to make You my best friend that You would bless me with five amazing friends. Thank you so much for Tam, Lance, Amanda, Brian, and even Nic. They aren't the friends I would have chosen, but

You know so much better than I do what I need. Please help us to focus on You individually, and as a group. Help each of us to realize Your way and Your timing are always best, God. I love You.

Nic's text for the morning message was two-fold. The first part was found in *Luke 17:4, And if he trespass against thee seven times in a day, and seven times in a day turn again to thee, saying, I repent; thou shalt forgive him.* And the second was in *Romans 5:20, Moreover the law entered, that the offence might about. But where sin abounded, grace did much more abound.*

"How many people, by a show of hands, have ever had anyone ask your forgiveness? Okay. Looks like everyone in this room. Again, by a show of hands, how many people have given that forgiveness? Just about everyone." Nic said with a chuckle. "A couple of you don't look too sure." Good natured pokes and jabs were being passed between friends and siblings.

Nic asked another question. "Please don't raise your hands, but how many of you have been asked to forgive someone and you refused that forgiveness?" He waited several moments to allow people time to think. "What did that person do to you that was so bad and hateful that you refused to forgive them?" He paused again.

"Let me ask another question. Again, please nobody raise your hand. How many of you, sitting here in these pews this morning, have done something even worse to someone than that person did to you?" Once again he paused to allow the words to ferment a little in everyone's minds. "If we were raising our hands, every hand in here ought to be raised."

Nic stuck his hand in his pocket and walked out to side of the pulpit, "You say, 'Pastor Nic, you don't know what this person did to me!' You're right. I don't know. Maybe you're thinking, 'You wouldn't forgive them either, Preacher, if you were in my position.' Well, maybe not. But it's not about what I would do, is it?"

Silence fell across the congregation as we each pondered the truth Nic was presenting.

"How many times a day do we all offend *someone,* and we don't even stop to say we're sorry *or* to ask forgiveness? Hold on. Hold on. I see those minds a reeling."

Nic took a deep breath and moved out from behind the pulpit as he continued. "I'm not talking about a coworker, or a spouse, or a brother or sister; I'm talking about God. How many times a day do we sin against the God of the universe, the One who created us, the One who died for the very sins we commit each and every day? We lie. We cheat. We wish bad things would happen to that neighbor who plays their music too loud."

We all chuckled a bit uneasily.

"All of us offend God every day of our lives. Some may think, 'Oh, it's not *that* bad. It's just a little *white* lie.' Hmm. Is that so? Well, what about in the Bible where is says to let your yea be yea and your nay, nay? It doesn't say to let your yea be 'well, you see, what happened was….' and your nay be 'the Devil made me do it'. A lie is a lie the same as murder is murder. In God's eyes, every sin is an offense to His holiness, no matter what 'level' of bad we've assigned to it."

Nic looked thoughtfully at his Bible. "The truth is folks, none of us deserves to be forgiven. Not one of us here this morning deserves to be loved by a Holy God. No one in this room is worthy of the grace God extends to each of us on a daily basis, but He still gives it to us – and He gives it freely. You see, it's not about what I would do in your situation; it's about asking ourselves what God would do were He faced with the same choices we're faced with."

"Perhaps someone here is thinking that it's easier for God to give grace than it is for us to give grace. Not so. In order for God to give His grace to you to cover your filthy hidden sin, it cost Him the life of His only Son, Jesus Christ. He had to die to give you grace. What does grace cost you? A little bit of pride. Maybe squelching your selfishness for a bit. You certainly aren't required to die in order to forgive someone."

"Maybe you're here this morning thinking, 'Well, they just don't deserve forgiveness. I'm willing and ready to forgive, but they just don't deserve it.' Um. Have you met God?"

Chuckles were heard across the auditorium.

"God isn't a respecter of persons, nor does He withhold His forgiveness from anyone. When He died on the cross to pay for our sins, He died for the *entire* world all at once. Salvation is free to *anyone* who asks for it. God's grace is sufficient for *everybody's* sin – not just mine."

"So your neighbor backed over your dog – big deal! You probably had a fleeting unkind thought about them when it happened. Your sin against God requires way more forgiveness and grace than their accidently killing your dog requires. Your sin is against a holy and righteous God. Their offense is toward a vile and wretched sinner, saved by grace. You don't deserve the grace of God, but He offers it to you freely in spite of all your sin."

"In our text in *Romans*, it tells us the Law is there so sin can abound. What that means is that with the Law in place, we can clearly see what's wrong and what right. The Law leaves no wiggle room in identifying our sin. But God doesn't leave it at that. He says that where the Law is, sin abounds, and where sin abounds it's fertile ground for His grace to abound even more. We're able to experience more grace because His Word reveals to us our sin; we confess our sin to a holy God, and we become the recipients of undeserved grace."

"You say, 'Okay. I get that. I don't deserve grace, but God gives it to me anyway. But what does *Luke* have to do with anything? All that forgiving someone seven times and all that; I don't get that.' Okay. Let's think about this. Who are we supposed to follow? Whose example are we as Christians to look to for guidance?"

Everyone in the auditorium was still as we contemplated what Nic was going to say next. We all knew the answer to the question; it was the answer every child in kids' church gave when they didn't know the right answer but they wanted to say something – *Jesus*. None of us wanted to think of the effect that one answer ought to have on our lives.

"We all know the answer." Nic said. "It's *Jesus*. His example is laid out in the Bible so that we can follow Him. We are to study His life and His ministry and strive to be like Christ. The ultimate example of His forgiveness in my opinion is when He was on the cross and looking to Heaven. With His last breath, He asked God to forgive the very people who were spitting on Him, beating Him, piercing Him with spears, and laughing at Him. His only thought as He hung on the cross was grace – the unmerited favor of God being extended to unworthy and ungrateful humanity."

"What is your first thought when someone offends you? What are your feelings toward the sins you see in other people's lives? Do you pray for them? Or do you look at them and judge them? How about when you see how someone close to you treats other people and how they seem to get away with horrendous things and never seem to be repentant or feel guilt on any level? Do you forgive them?"

"You say, 'They didn't ask me to forgive them, so I don't have to.' Is that what Christ said on the cross? Did He wait for the masses to ask forgiveness before He asked God to give it to them? No. He made sure He did the right thing, even though they did not."

"People won't always ask your forgiveness, but you ought to forgive them anyway. Even if they keep on offending and keep on offending you, you need to forgive – whether they ask you to do so or not, you *must* forgive. Follow Christ's example. You say, 'It's not easy, Preacher!' I know. Believe me, I know. I'm a man, a *hu-man* just like you! But we are to be like Christ and He's not exactly known for choosing the easy route, now is He. And He has it a whole lot harder than you ever will! He has to give grace to your sorry carcass; all you have to do is forgive your husband for eating your secret ice cream stash for a midnight snack."

Husbands and wives looked at other; some smiled, some chuckled, and others looked grim.

"It is foolish for us to think we can decide who deserves grace and who doesn't. It's not up to us, folks. We are to give forgiveness in our hearts even before anyone asks for it. Let's pray."

177

Brian seemed preoccupied after the morning service and decided to go back to the house. Tam said she needed to run an errand and asked Amanda if she'd like to ride along with her and grab a bite of lunch. The two of them took off and left Lance and I standing in the aisle of the church alone. Nic came walking into the back of the auditorium from the lobby.

"Hey, you two! How are you?"

"Doing well, thanks." I answered. "How're you, Nic?"

"Fantastic. That's great news about Tam! She told me in the lobby today!" He said with a smile.

"Yeah! I was in shock when she told me, to be honest." I admitted. "I feel so guilty for living under the same roof with her for so long and just assuming she was already saved because she was reading the Bible and going to church."

Nic was nodding. "Well, don't feel too bad, Nel. A lot of Christians do the same thing. We focus so much on our own outward shows of Christianity that we begin to mistake church attendance and such for true salvation. Anyone can go to church and do all the right things without actually being saved."

"That's true," Lance jumped in. "I grew up in church and was really involved in the children's ministry back East before I realized I wasn't saved. I was sixteen and a leader in the youth group when I humbled myself and accepted Christ."

"A lot of people never come to that point, Lance." Nic said. "That's great that you did. Now we just need to get the rest of the Christians saved and we'll be in business!"

Lance laughed his loud belly laugh that had at one time embarrassed me. It didn't seem so loud anymore. "Right on, Preacher." His head bobbed up and down. I grinned.

"Oh! Nic!"

"Oh! Nelia!" Nic responded with feigned enthusiasm, mocking my spastic manifestation of my memory kicking in. I stuck my tongue out at him.

"I *was* going to invite you to dinner tomorrow night but now I'm not so sure with that attitude...."

"Oh, I can play the part of a gentleman when I have to." Nic winked and then glanced at Lance. Lance just grinned.

"Nic. We'd love to have you come to my house tomorrow night." Lance spoke up. "Nel is cooking up something special for Tam, Brian, Amanda, and me. You'd make it an even six if you came and everything's always better in evens."

Nic's brow furrowed. "I thought you were always supposed to do things in odd numbers."

"Well when it comes to food the more the merrier. Right, Nel?"

"Of course. Will you come, Nic?"

"I suppose." He grinned. "I *am* single after all. A home-cooked meal is always welcome!"

Monday evening found the six of us gathered around Lance's dining room table, enjoying a meal of tender pot roast with chunks of potatoes, carrots, and onions cooked to perfection. I had made homemade biscuits and they were perfectly flaky; my mom would have been proud.

Somehow, the conversation had turned into everyone taking turns telling our stories. Nic went first and told us all about his upbringing in Seattle, Washington and about college life and his experiences as a volunteer paramedic. I was next and shared how God had brought me to California in search of a house just like the one in which we sat so I could start my book shop.

"I didn't know that." Lance said.

"Yeah. If I could find the twin of your house I would be a happy woman!"

"Interesting." Was all he responded.

It was Lance's turn. He began by telling us about the accident that had set his and Amanda's lives on the only course either of them had ever known. I noticed Brian was focused intently on what Lance was saying. His jaw clenched tightly.

"I remember sitting in the hospital with my grandparents, wondering if Amanda was going to make it. It didn't really sink in for a while that my parents were both gone. Even now, almost nineteen years later, it's hard for me to drive on Highway 50 on the east side of Cambridge. Just one of those things I suppose."

Brian interrupted. "Wait. You said Highway 50?"

"Yeah."

"East of Cambridge?"

"Uh huh. Why?"

He sat quietly for a moment. "And you said this was almost nineteen years ago?"

"Yeah." Replied Lance. "It'll be nineteen years August twenty-seventh."

Brian's brow was creased deeply. He looked as if he were piecing together some complicated, intricate, and immensely important puzzle. Suddenly, I heard him gasp, "There's no way!" He jumped up from his chair and ran out of the room.

We all sat in stunned silence for a moment before it hit me what was happening.

"I'll go." I jumped up and followed him. I found him on the front porch, leaning against the rail with his head down. I could see his face was red but he wasn't crying.

"Brian?"

"Go away, Nel."

"What's going on?"

"I don't want to talk about it!"

"You *have* to." I said. "You cannot storm out of a room like that and just expect me to drop it. Now what's going on?"

Brian turned his back to me. He drew several very deep breaths and exhaled slowly each time. He hung his head again. "I just can't believe it. This can't be happening" he mumbled.

"What, Brian?" I pressed. "What can't be happening?"

He turned to me slowly, his hands hanging helplessly at his sides. He looked forlorn and helpless. I had no idea what was coming.

"The accident, Nel. It was my dad. My dad was the drunk driver! He killed their parents and put Amanda in that wheel chair!"

Laura Wagenschutz and W. Mark Dendy

CHAPTER 22

We stood in silence on the porch, just me and Brian, for what seemed like an eternity. A cool breeze floated across the porch and the moon hung in the South Eastern sky. I felt a sickness in my stomach, and I could not imagine what Brian was feeling. How could I explain to Brian the series of events that had occurred were all part of God's plan?

I quickly examined my own life up to that very moment in search of what to say, and I realized that I needed to rely on God, to trust Him to give me the words - words that may give Brian comfort.

I took my hand and gently wiped the tears from Brian's cheeks.

Brian covered his face with his hands. "What am I gonna do Nel? What can I do? What can I say? They'll never forgive me if they find out! How can all this be happening to me now? Now that I've turned my life over to Christ," Brian said with a muffled voice.

I could hear footsteps coming through the house. Nic stuck his head out the door and said, "Hey Nel. Tam's not feeling well. Can she take your car back to the apartment and Lance or I will take you home?"

The porch was dimly lit, but Nic could sense that Brian was in great despair. "Is everything alright?"

I motioned for Nic to go back inside and said, "Yeah. Everything's okay. Give us a few minutes. We'll be in shortly."

"What about Tam? Your car? Can she take it home?"

"Yeah. No problem. Keys are in my purse," I said, a bit annoyed.

I put my arms around Brian and pulled him to me and gently whispered a prayer.

"Father God, Ruler of all, I lift Brian up to You this night in this time of distress. Father we know as You say in *Isaiah 55* that Your ways are not our ways and Your thoughts are not our thoughts, but Lord You also say in *Matthew 7,* ask and it shall be given unto you and to seek and we shall find."

The door opened and Tam walked past us down the steps and straight to my car. As she crossed the porch, she whispered, "Thanks Nel. See ya Brian."

Tam started the car and pulled down the driveway, and I continued praying, "Lord God Almighty we ask for wisdom in how to deal with this delicate situation, how to both ask and give forgiveness and we seek to find that peace that passeth all understanding Lord. Be with each one of us this evening as we try to see and understand our purpose both individually and collectively. In Jesus precious name. Amen and Amen."

While I prayed, I felt Brian's muscle tense up as he attempted to subdue his crying. When I finished we were both holding each other closely, like a brother and a sister would hold each other at the loss of a friend or loved one.

Brian looked at me and said, "Thanks Nel. Thank you so much for praying with me. I guess I'm still at a loss at what to say to Lance and Amanda. I don't see how they can forgive me when I can't forgive my dad, and *he's my dad!*"

"Would you like me to get Nic out here so you can talk to him? Maybe he can give you some guidance. After all he is a pastor."

"I need a little time to think about this, maybe try and pray about it. You go back inside. I'll be in in a bit."

"Are you sure you're okay by yourself?"

"Yeah. I'll be okay, and besides, I'm not by myself. Right Nel?"

"I'm happy to hear you say that. You know He'll never leave you."

"I know that now. Just wish I had of known that all my life. Things would have been easier, might have been different for us, you and me."

"Brian. They might have, but God has a perfect plan for you and one for me too; let's don't second guess that."

I kissed Brian on the cheek and went inside.

I sat down at the table, and there was an uneasiness lingering in the room. Nic broke the silence with, "Is everything alright? How is Brian?"

"He's struggling. He has a huge burden, one that only God can lift off his shoulders," I said.

"I'm going to go out and talk to him," Lance said as he pushed back his chair from the table.

"I don't think that's a good idea," I said.

Nic piped in immediately, "Nel's probably right. Let's give him a little more time. If he isn't at the table in five minutes, I'll go out and talk with him."

Lance was reluctant but said, "Okay, but I've got a sick feeling about what's going on."

Amanda was sitting silent with tears streaming down her cheeks. She had managed to mash the potatoes, onions and carrots left on her plate with her fork to the point they were indistinguishable.

"What is going on Lance. Tell me! Where is this God of yours now?" Her obvious sadness had turned quickly to anger.

"Come on Sis. Don't talk like that. God is here and he is dealing with Brian right now."

"But what about me? Who's gonna deal with me and my hurts? Huh?"

"He's here, and He is going to help you deal with your hurts and me with mine. You just have to trust Him Amanda. He is bigger than all our problems!" Lance reached across the table and took Amanda's hands in his. She pulled back.

"God will work everything out. You will find joy in Him."

While Lance consoled Amanda, Nic and I quietly left the room and went to the entry way. I turned to Nic and said, "Let me go out first and see how Brian's doing. I'll come back in a get you if he wants to talk to you."

"Wait a second Nel," Nic said grabbing my wrist and turning me to him. "What is going on?"

"Oh. Right. You don't know."

"Does it have anything to do with Lance's story at dinner?"

"It has everything to do with Lance's story. Brian's dad was the drunk driver caused the accident."

Nic put his hand over his mouth and gasped. "I have to go out and talk to Brian, pray with him."

"Just wait Nic. Let me go see if he's ready."

I walked out on the porch. Brian wasn't there. I called out for him in a low voice so that Lance and Amanda wouldn't be able to hear me. I descended the five wooden steps quietly to the front yard and called out for Brian again, a little louder. No response. The moon was waxing three quarters and cast an even glow on the uneven ground that surrounded the house. I walked all the way around the house calling Brian's name. He was gone.

I rushed back to the front and dashed up the steps into the house. I was breathing rapidly and fell into Nic's arms as I opened the door.

"He's gone," I said to Nic as I caught my breath.

"Gone?"

"Yes. As in nowhere to be found! What should we do?" I said.

Lance came rushing out of the dining room and stopped right in front of me.

"Nel," he said, "You have to tell me what's going on."

I looked at Nic and then back at Lance. Before I could speak Lance said, "Brian's father was the one that killed my parents, wasn't he?"

"Oh gosh Lance. I'm so sorry," I said.

"It's not your fault Nel. Why would you say you're sorry? Have you known about this all along?"

I sensed a tinge of anger in Lance's voice.

"Of course not. I just found out tonight. And Brian just realized it when you were telling the story," I said a bit defensively.

"Tell Brian to come in and we'll work through this together. God didn't set us on this course to feel sorry for ourselves. This new revelation actually will bring some closure to Amanda and me, and we will be able to put Pastor Nic's sermon to use."

Nic and I stood there speechless as we observed God working through Lance.

"Now go get Brian Nel, and tell him to come back inside," Lance said.

"He's not here," I said.

"What do you mean, he's not here?" Lance asked.

"I mean he, he was on the porch when I went inside but now he's gone. I looked all around the yard."

Brian's rental car was still in the driveway. The house was surrounded by dense woods on both sides and the back. The driveway ran down the hill to the main road some 300 yards away.

"What should we do?" I asked looking to both Nic and Lance for some direction.

Lance said, "Let me get Amanda to her bedroom and we'll go out and look for Brian."

"Should I stay here with Amanda?" I asked Lance.

"That's probably a good idea. She really admires you Nel," Lance replied.

Nic said, "Let's pray for some direction first."

Lance said, "Good idea Pastor."

We formed a circle and grasped hands. Nic's and Lance's hands swallowed up my hands, and I could feel the warmth from each of their hearts flow towards me as Nic prayed.

"God of Abraham, Isaac, and Jacob. We ask that you forgive us of our trespasses against one another and against You Father, and we ask that You gives us each a forgiving heart. And Lord, we especially ask You to be with Brian in this time of need and Lord give us direction in how we should search for him. We put our faith and our trust in You Lord. Amen."

Lance and Nic searched the woods surrounding the house and drove up and down the road five miles south of the property and north as far as town, but to no avail. Nic tried calling Brian's cell phone, but each time it rolled over to voicemail. Nic left a couple of messages.

Lance had told Amanda when he took her to her bedroom the news about Brian's revelation. Amanda lay on her bed and I sat beside her. I stroked her hair as she sobbed. I didn't know what to say and even if I did I probably wouldn't know how to say it, so I just sat there silently hoping and praying that my physical presence and my touch would comfort her. Then it was if God layed everything out for me. Three scriptures came to mind that I had committed to memory and I shared them with Amanda. As I recited each scripture she turned to them in her Bible and highlighted them with a pink highlighter.

For my thoughts are not your thoughts, neither are your ways my ways, saith the LORD. Isaiah 55:8

There are many devices in a man's heart; nevertheless the counsel of the LORD, that shall stand. Proverbs 19:21

For I know the thoughts that I think toward you, saith the LORD, thoughts of peace, and not of evil, to give you an expected end. Jeremiah 29:11

She said it still didn't make sense to her, and she asked me to pray so she could understand.

I didn't hesitate for even a moment. Sitting on the bed beside her I took her hand in mine and began. "Our heavenly Father. I cannot begin to understand the pain that Amanda feels, but You know and understand her intimately because Your Word tells us that before Amanda was formed in her mother's womb You had a plan and a purpose for her life. We don't know what the plan is, but Lord You say to cast our cares on You, that You will bear our burdens, and Lord this has got to be a crushing burden on Amanda and I ask in the name of Jesus, Your Son and our Savior that you take this burden from Amanda. In Jesus precious name…"

Before I could say "amen" Amanda said, "And God… I'm not so good at praying, but I want to thank you for bringing Nel into my life. I don't know where I would be without her, if she hadn't led me back to You, I would probably be ready to kill myself. Lord, I love her as a sister and thank You so much for her, and Lord God, please help me understand why all this has happened in my life and help me to trust more in You and please take the pain away and give me the kind of peace that Nel has. In my precious Savior Jesus' name. Amen."

"Amen!" Lance and Nic said in unison. They had been standing in the doorway listening to us send our requests up to heaven.

"Did you find him?" I asked.

"Nope. No luck," Nic said.

"Find who?" Amanda said, apparently oblivious to the fact that Brian was gone and Nic and Lance had been out searching for him. It was now after midnight.

"Brian. He left but we don't know where he went," Lance said.

"How long ago did he leave?" Amanda queried.

"We're not sure, but before I brought you into your room," Lance said.

"Oh no. Oh my gosh!" Amanda said her tanned face went pale.

"What? Amanda. What are you thinking?" I said.

"He's blaming himself for what his dad did, and I bet he thinks we won't be able to forgive him. Go get my cell phone Lance."

"What are you going to do Amanda?" I asked.

She looked up at Nic as if she were looking for guidance. "What were those two scriptures you had in yesterday's sermon?"

Nic pulled his Blackberry out of his pocket and scrolled through it and dropped his phone back in his pocket. He said, "*Luke 17:4* and…"

"Hold on, hold on." Amanda said. She turned in her Bible to the verse just as Lance returned with her phone. Lance handed her the phone and she began texting.

Hey brian its Amanda. member the sermon yesterday? if he trespass against 7 times n a day

I had caught on to her plan and I took her bible out of her lap and said, "Let me help. I'll read. You text. Okay. Where were you?" I asked.

"Read it from the beginning."

"Ok. *And if he trespass against thee seven times in a day, and seven times in a day turn again to thee, saying, I repent; thou shalt forgive him.*"

Her fingers were moving so quickly it seemed that by the time the last word had left my lips she had pressed *send*.

"Okay Pastor. What was the other…"

"*Romans 5:20,*" Nic said. He had waited in anticipation.

I quickly thumbed the pages three books over and place my finger on the verse. "Ready?" I asked looking at Amanda.

"Go," was all she said.

"*Moreover the law entered, that the offence might about. But where sin abounded, grace did much more abound,*" I read as Amanda entered an abbreviated version into her phone and hit *send*. She had not received a reply from the first text.

She entered another text as tears formed in her eyes.

Brian grace and forgiveness will abound in your life and ours. Please just give us a chance. Please come back.

We waited for Amanda to get a reply for what seemed like an eternity. Finally Nic said, "I'm going to try and call him again." It was 12:55 a.m.

Nic pulled his phone back out of his pocket. There were three text messages – all from Amanda's phone.

Just as he realized what had happened, the doorbell rang.

Lance darted for the front door, and I was right on his heels.

Lance opened the door and two CHP officers stood on the porch, one in front of the door, the other to his right with his hand resting in the ready position on his firearm.

"Are you Lance Dupont?"

"Yes officer," Lance said. By then Nic was standing looking over Lance's shoulder. That made the officers a tad antsy.

"Would you step outside please?"

"No problem officer. What's going on?"

"Close the door behind you please."

Lance closed the door, but Nic and I were still able to make out what was being said.

"We have a fellow that we picked up wandering aimlessly along Highway 49 about seven and a half miles south of here. He appeared distraught. We thought maybe he was on drugs or under the influence of alcohol, but we checked him out, and he was stone cold sober. He said he had gotten some bad news tonight and was trying to figure things out. His identification shows he's an out-of-stater, but he said he lived here."

"Yes officer. He does."

"Well then we'll leave him with you."

The two officers went to their patrol car and opened the back door. Brian stepped out of the car. The officers turned the car around and left. Brian just stood still, staring at the ground. He took a couple of steps toward the porch, then stopped. Nic and I had opened the door, but stood there as if frozen in time.

Lance began to descend the steps to his porch. Nic and I both took a deep breath, and then we watched God at work. Lance paused at the second step from the top then leaped to the ground and ran the short distance to where Brian had begun to fall to his knees. Lance caught him and picked him up embracing him with all the brotherly love and forgiveness that man can only find through God's grace.

Nic and I stood as we watched Lance and Brian hugging and weeping together. Nic put his arm around me, and I rested my head on his shoulder. Then Nic looked upwards and said in a whisper, "Your will be done. Praise God."

"Praise God!"

CHAPTER 23

Amanda was waiting patiently in her bedroom. Almost an hour had passed before Brian knocked quietly on her door.

"Come in,"she called out tentatively.

Brian slowly opened the door and stood with his hands hanging at his sides. His talk with Lance had bolstered his hope that Amanda might not hold his father's wrong against him, but in the back of his mind he seriously doubted either of them could ever forgive him or his father completely. He stood there quietly staring at the floor for a long while.

Amanda broke the silence. "You gonna stand there forever?"

"I don't know." Brian shrugged. "Maybe."

"Well, I can't come to you, silly," Amanda chuckled.

Brian walked slowly to the edge of the bed and sunk to his knees. Resting his elbows on the bed he looked up into Amanda's eyes, "Could you ever forgive me, Amanda? I know I don't deserve it and I know you don't have to give it, but I do want you to know I'm sorry for what my father did to you. You don't deserve all the pain he's caused you. You didn't deserve to lose your parents. I won't blame you if you hate me."

"Shhh!" Amanda pressed her finger to his lips. "I don't deserve to be alive," Brian, she said with a somber voice. "God allowed the accident to happen and He chose that time to take my parents for whatever reason. He also chose to allow me to live in this wheelchair for a reason. He's God. His way is absolutely perfect and us questioning His method only causes us to become bitter, Brian. That's not what God wants! It's not your fault that the Devil has your dad tricked into believing he needs the alcohol; your dad has chosen that path, not you. And I'm not angry at your dad either. He's in bondage to alcohol and he's living a miserable life, haunted by thoughts of what could have been and by regrets of what has been. I don't blame him. There is no benefit to holding that grudge anymore. I've held it for so long and allowed it to have power over my life, but not anymore. God's given me grace to get through it and some extra grace to pass around to those I've been holding grudges against."

Brian's head was buried in his hands. He was weeping.

"Let it go, Brian."

"It's not that easy!" He practically shouted as he quickly raised his eyes to look at Amanda. "You have no idea what he's done. He paid people off, Amanda, in order to get out of what he deserved for killing your parents. He's done it multiple times on different levels and he always gets away with it because he has money. He pushed my mom to the point of becoming suicidal and disowned me for following his example in my business dealings. He's evil. How do you forgive someone like that?"

Amanda wasn't sure how to respond. *Lord, I know I asked for a chance to show Your love and forgiveness to someone but this might be too big a challenge for me. I don't know if I'm ready for this! Brian has a deep bitterness — dare I say hatred — for his father. How could I possibly help him?*

She could feel the presence of God in the room and suddenly knew what to say.

"Brian," began Amanda. "Do you know the story about the blind man in the Bible? The one where people were asking why he was blind and everything?"

"Yeah."

"Why was he blind? What was the purpose?"

Brian thought for a moment. "So God could get the glory, right?"

"Right!" Amanda clapped in excitement. "God had a reason for making him blind that no one else could see or understand! But when God's timing was perfect, His will was fulfilled and a valuable lesson was learned. Right?"

"Yeah. Well... I guess so." Brian was thinking.

"It's the same with everything in life. Things happen. People do things that make us mad. Those we love hurt us. Total strangers rip away the lives of those we love for what appears to be no reason at all; but God is still God. He allows these thing in order to teach us to wait on Him and to trust Him. In His time, He will be glorified in every aspect of our lives if we'll trust Him."

Brian remained quietly kneeling at the side of the bed. Amanda could tell his heart was heavy and that he was pondering everything she'd said.

"I don't know." Brian sighed a sigh that seemed to come from the bottom of his soul. "I just don't know, Amanda. I'm really gonna have to do some thinking. And praying too I guess."

"Good idea, Brian." She smiled. "I'll be praying for you too!"

The next few days were quiet for all of us. We tried to keep things light when we were together, but I think we were all feeling a great amount of emotional stress for Brian. In the very short time he'd been in Jackson, our little group had embraced him. None of us really knew how to help him; even Nic was somewhat at a loss. Nic and Brian had met for coffee a couple times since Monday night, but by Saturday morning, Brian was still carrying the weight of his father's sins on his shoulders and in his countenance.

Lance and I had been spending quite a bit of time together praying for Brian and talking about the struggles Amanda was facing – both physically and emotionally. She was taking the news well, but the doctors said they could tell she was under a lot of stress because she had relapsed in some of her physical therapy. I could feel myself being drawn to Lance more and more and was uncertain of a proper course of action. I knew Lance liked me, but what I was feeling was turning into more than simply liking him. I felt my heart growing more attached to him with each passing day.

Part of me felt that I was betraying God by allowing myself to have feelings for Lance after having made my commitment to God to be single, while the other part of me was saying that God brought Lance into my life, and it was up to Him to get him out if he wasn't the one for me. I was confused on many levels. I needed to talk to my sister.

Rachel picked up on the second ring. "Hey, sis! Long time, no talk! What's going on with you?"

"Oh my. Maybe it would be easier to answer what's *not* going on with me."

"Okaaaay…" She drawled. "What's *not* going on with you?"

"Well, I haven't lost my job at the travel agency."

"Uh huh?"

"And I am most definitely *not* pregnant!"

"What?!" Rachel screeched. "You had better be teasing about that even being a possibility, Nel, or so help me I will get on a plane right now and come rip out your lady parts in sisterly love!"

"Oh wow! Calm down, Rach. It's not even a possibility; trust me."

"Good." I could hear her take a deep breath. "Don't you ever do that to me again!"

I laughed. Rachel didn't find it humorous at all. "Sorry. I won't do it again."

"Good. Now what's *actually* going on in your life?"

I proceeded to tell her about the progression of events over the past few weeks since we'd last spoken; everything from Brian's arrival and salvation to my confusion and guilt concerning my developing feelings for Lance. I couldn't remember a time when I'd been able to talk to my sister without being interrupted. Rachel's hubby had taken the kids to the park when he realized our conversation had a bit more to it than shoes and swapping recipes.

Brother-in-laws aren't all that bad, I guess.

"Hmmm." Rachel took a moment to organize her thoughts. "Okay, sis, here's the dealio. You've gotta let Brian go. Yes, God brought him back into your life, but He's not handing him to you on a silver platter while the heavenly hosts sing *The Wedding March*. God has His reasons for Brian being there – one of which was see him saved. Don't let your mind get ahead of God and try reading into things that aren't even there. Tam getting saved is huge, but she's still got a ton of growing to do; that's where you come in. God brought the two of you together for a reason, Nel. You have to help Tam as God begins working on her and showing her what she needs to change. It's not gonna be easy, but you have to do it. Amanda is a bit harder to figure out. I think she's part way there on the forgiveness thing, but she's young and God is still working on her. Give her a little space, but don't back down when God hands you an opportunity to step in and guide her."

"How do I know when it's God handing me an opportunity though, Rachel?"

"You'll know. It'll just feel right. I promise."

"Okay." I sighed. "If you say so."

"Yeah. Now. Nic seems to be growing a lot since the first time you met him. If I remember correctly, you pretty much despised the man. Am I right?"

I giggled. "Well, yeah. Maybe. Just a little though!"

"Well whatever. You couldn't stand the man. But from what you're telling me, God is working on him and changing him in only ways God knows how. I, personally, don't think he's right for Tam but I'm not God. We'll leave that up to Him to decide later."

"Yeah. I'm not too sure on that one either."

"Yeah. Just wait and God'll work that one out. Now. The juicy stuff." I could almost envision Rachel sitting in the middle of her living room floor, folding laundry; I saw the same mischievous glint in her eye that she'd had when we were children. "About Lance…"

"Yeah?" I half-way wondered if I really wanted to know what she was going to say.

"You're gonna marry him."

"What?!" It was my turn to nearly drop the phone.

"Well, not like tomorrow or anything!"

"But you can't just *saaaaay* something like that and move on!"

Rachel paused. "I just did, didn't I?"

The conversation with my sister had left me reeling. I knew I liked Lance a lot but I was not sure he was the one for me. Nic was still the perfect option, but he didn't seem interested. Brian wasn't even in the running. I sat on my little patio, sipping coffee and talking to God.

What is wrong with me, God? Why can't You just make it obvious who I should date – if anyone? That would make my life so much easier! I don't want to tell You how to do Your job, but… could You maybe step it up just a tad on the whole enlightenment thing? Because I've been sitting here confused for a while, and getting to the point where I'm emotionally drained. I just want to please You with my life. I'd really like a boyfriend, but if I haven't learned to depend solely on You, then please just give me the patience I need to keep waiting for the right guy to come along.

I heard a knock at the door.

"Coming!" I shouted in a sing-song manner as I quickly set my coffee cup down and made my way to the door. Brian stood on the other side with a smile spread across his face.

"Hey!" I greeted him. "What's going on?"

"I got the job! The job with Chase Bank! I'll be moving on Tuesday!"

"What?" I exclaimed. "That soon?"

"Yeah. They said they need me to start right away!"

I stood in stunned silence for a moment. "Well, that's great, Brian! It's really, really soon, but I'm happy for you!"

"Can you help me find a place? I know you're really good with all those real estate sites; I thought maybe you'd at least be able to point me in the right direction or something."

"Sure! Of course." I opened the door wide and invited him in. Before I could close the door, Lance pulled into the parking space right next to Brian's car. He waved as he climbed out of his Camaro.

"Hey, Nel." Lance flashed me a smile. "What's happening?"

"Brian just got here. He's got some news; do you want to come in?"

"Sure!" Lance brushed past me leaving in his wake the tantalizing scent of his musky cologne.

Oh, Lord, help me!

The three of us spent the remainder of the afternoon pouring over real estate websites, looking for a house or apartment for Brian to rent. The conversation somehow turned to my dream of opening *Penny a Page* and my tireless pursuit of the perfect house for it.

"She's wanted to do this basically for forever." Brian said.

"That's great, Nel!" Lance's head was bobbing up and down excitedly. "You should *totally* do it!"

"Well, I will! Just as soon as I can save up the money for the house and the renovations I'm sure will have to be done before I can open up."

"That shouldn't be too much though, right?" Lance said.

"It's more than you think."

"Hm." I could tell Lance's mind was working but I didn't ask questions. "Interesting."

CHAPTER 24

I didn't give any more thought to Lance's waxing curiosity about my *Penny a Page* dream. I was caught up in helping Brian not only find a place to live in or around San Francisco, but also helping him find a way to forgive his father and make amends while his father was still alive. I had grown to love Brian in a very different way as we drove back and forth to the North Bay area to find him a new home, and we shared in the excitement of him getting a fresh start.

A little over two weeks had passed since our Monday evening dinner that ripped open the hearts of all the my now very dear friends, and it was evident that God was at work in each one of us in very different ways. He was remaking us like clay in the Potter's hand, mending our tears and fixing our flaws.

It was a Wednesday and I had taken the afternoon off to run to Vallejo with Brian to look at a loft apartment overlooking the Carquinez Strait. Despite the 90 plus degree weather, there was a cool delta breeze blowing as we stepped out onto the patio. A couple of sailboats were out on the glistening water. Brian turned to the property manager and said, "I'll take it. It's perfect!" Then he pushed his Ray Ban shades down to the bottom of his nose so I could see his eyes and he said, "Nel, I never thought life could be so good without you being my girlfriend."

"What?" I was stunned. "What do you *mean* life could be so good without me as your girlfriend?"

I punched at him with both fists and he caught my hands in mid-air.

"No, no Nel. I didn't mean it that way. I meant I didn't know things could be so good with you as just my friend – not as my girlfriend."

My right brow was raised and my lips were pursed.

"Really, Nel. The words just came out wrong. I swear."

I tried to maintain the tough girl image but couldn't and burst out laughing. Brian chuckled a little, but I could tell he was concerned that he might have really hurt my feelings.

"That's okay Brian. Go ahead. Just rip my heart out and stomp on it, why don't you?" I said as I put on a charade as though I was ripping my own heart out. I then stomped on the ground and shouted, "Take that you beast. Take that!"

The property manager had stood patiently watching us and probably wondered whether she should rent to someone that could very well be a runaway from a nut house.

She looked at me disapprovingly and then at Brian and said, "The deposit is $2000 and you can move in as soon as you like. We take cash or check."

Brian looked at the woman and then at me and said in a lousy Texas drawl, "Pay the woman, honey."

"I forgot the chickens we were planning to trade, dear." I responded dryly.

"Oh. Well, in that case," he reached into his pocket and pulled out his wallet, "I suppose I'll have to cover it this time."

"Yeah, I guess so." I chuckled.

We hopped in the car and headed back to Jackson hoping to make it through Sacramento before rush hour. It was a two and a half hour drive back to Jackson in light traffic, and Brian and I both wanted to make it back for church service.

I was listening to the radio station K-Love and Brian was singing. A song came on with a catchy tune and I recognized it right away. It was *Avalon's A Maze of Grace*. I turned up the volume and said, "Listen, listen Brian. You'll love this song."

I sang with the radio at the top of my lungs:

I run, I fall, I walk, I sometimes crawl
I give, I take, I bend and yet somehow I break
I get dizzy from all this spinning 'round
I'm determined but wonder where I'm bound
I've learned to follow the sweet familiar sound of Your voice

The straight and narrow twists and turns
I make my way and everyday
I live I learn to follow You
You walk me through a maze of grace

I stand, I sway, I reach for You, I push away
I'm spent, I'm saved, I disobey yet I behave
In my personal struggle to break free
The only peace for the puzzle that I need
Is just to follow the sweet familiar lead of Your love

The straight and narrow twists and turns
I make my way and everyday
I live I learn to follow You
You walk me through a maze of grace

I'm lost in you and there I'm found
You're gently guiding
Every time I turn around it's no surprise
To see my life's a maze of grace

Traffic was heavy so I was really paying attention to the road. When the song ended, I turned the radio down and said, "Isn't that a great song?"

I glanced over at Brian. Tears were running down his cheeks. His face was all pinched up as if he could hide the fact from me that the song had touched him. The Lord had really changed Brian, and I could tell that Brian was yielding to God.

I tried joking to cheer him up. "Was my singing *that* bad?"

He laughed through his tears, and then he looked at me and said, "That song says it all, Nel, in such simple words – my life really is a maze of grace."

"Amen to that!"

"Thanks a lot!" he feigned indignation.

"No, you know what I meant!" I stuck my tongue out at Brian. "We're all in the same boat; it's not just you, silly."

"Oh sure. I know what you really meant."

"Whatever." We both chuckled.

It was six o'clock by the time we made it through Sacramento and I was headed out Highway 16 - Jackson Road. We both needed to change before church so I pushed my already leaden foot down a little harder on the accelerator. *After all*, I thought, *God wouldn't be mad at me for speeding a little to make it to church on time.*

The road was wide open as were my eyes when I looked up in the rear view mirror and saw red and blue flashing lights coming up quickly from the rear. I slowed down hoping that the law enforcement vehicle was in pursuit of an actual law breaking person and would sail right on by me. No such luck.

Brian sat beside me, his shoulders shaking as he attempted to stifle his laughter. He always did find enjoyment in my predicaments. I slapped him on the arm.

"Stop it! This is *not* funny, loser!"

"Yes! It is funny actually." He was no longer trying to hide anything. Brian's face was turning red, he was laughing so hard.

Really, Lord? Why tonight? I'm on the way to church for Pete's sake!

The CHP officer approached my car and I could see from my rear view mirror he looked vaguely familiar. I let down the passenger window as he walked cautiously up to the passenger side of the car. He leaned down and looked right past Brian directly at me.

"Ma'am. Did you know I clocked you doing 71 miles an hour back there in a 55 mile zone?"

"Well, officer," I said nervously, "I don't know for sure how fast I was going." I gulped hard.

"Could I see your license, registration, and insurance card?"

As the procedure for a traffic stop wasn't foreign to me, I had the documentation in my hand in anticipation.

He looked at everything then leaned down and looked through the window as if he had missed something.

"Hey. You're the guy that we found wandering outside of Jackson a couple of weeks ago. How are you doing man?"

"I'm doing okay," Brian said.

"Well. I've been praying for you. I don't know what your beliefs are, but if I didn't put my faith and trust in God, I wouldn't survive out here in this job."

The officer tipped his hat to Brian and then looked at me. "Now, as for you, Miss Nelia Chambers. It is Miss isn't it?"

"Yes," I said thinking, *Is it that obvious?*

"Even though you deserve a ticket for that lead foot of yours, I'm going to grant you a little grace this evening."

"Oh thank you so much, Officer."

"But don't you come driving through my roads all blazing like that again," he said as he handed my license and registration back.

I looked at Brian and grinned. Then I clasped my hands together looked up and mouthed the words *Thank You Lord.*

I quickly stole at glance at the officer through the side mirror as he walked back to his vehicle and wondered, but only for a brief moment, if he was single. I quickly dismissed the idea with the thought – *He's not my type.*

By the time we arrived in Jackson, we had missed the first twenty minutes or so of church. I said to Brian, "Why don't we just go to my apartment and talk about what I can do to help you get moved as quickly as possible so you aren't all stressed when Monday morning rolls around and your starting your big new job." I ended in a sing-song voice.

Brian said, "Okay. I know you are a list type of person so I will put you in charge of making a list and checking it twice."

Figaro was waiting for me when I opened the door and he followed me around until I fed him. I then put on a pot of coffee and made my way into the living room.

"Oh! I need a pen and paper." I remembered and skipped into my bedroom to retrieve the items. "Got them!" I announced as I found my way back to the living room. Kicking off my flip flops, I made myself comfortable at one end of the couch.

It was a hot August night and I thought, *Praise God we have air conditioning and it's working.*

"Okay, Brian. Why don't we go early Saturday morning to…"

"Wait, Nel. Before we start planning I want to ask you something. I need your advice. You know me better than I know myself most of the time so I would really like you to tell me what you think."

Brian was all jittery and nervous. I wasn't sure what was coming.

"Nel, I really like Amanda. I mean I really, really like her. I liked her the minute I met her."

"I know; I could tell. I was there. Remember, Brian?" I said with a touch of sarcasm.

"Well,…" he hesitated.
"Ask me, Brian. For crying out loud. Well what?" It had been a long day and I could feel the lack of caffeine starting to kick in; I was getting irritable.

"Do you think me and Amanda could be happy together? That is if she could ever like me enough to be with me. I mean… you know… with everything that's happened."

"I don't see why not."

"Really? Do you think so? I mean like we could have kids and all. You know I always wanted a big family."

"Whoa, Brian. Down boy!" I chuckled as I patted the top of his head. "Aren't you kind of putting the cart before the horse?"

"I don't know. Am I? Does it hurt to wonder? To dream?"

"No, it doesn't. But you need to be sure it's what God wants, Bri. Yeah, Amanda is gorgeous but there is a lot the two of you need to work out before you even think of a relationship. Maybe just be friends for now, huh?"

Brian hung his head. "Yeah, I guess you're right. I have a lot of learning and growing to do. The only model I've had for a husband and father isn't exactly the All-American type; I should probably learn what it means to be a Christian man before I try to be a Christian boyfriend."

"Very wise." I smiled. "And I'm ready to take you home because I just hit a wall, and you just reminded me that I need to be sure and get my eight hours of dreaming in tonight," I said as I yawned.

As we were headed out the door, Tam, Nic, and Lance came busting through the door pushing each other and laughing.

Tam headed for her room saying, "You guys made me laugh so hard I tinkled myself. I gotta change," she said holding her noise and mouth to curb her laughter.

"What's so funny?" I asked.

Tam yelled through her bedroom door, "Don't you tell her. I want to, because I'll tell it right."

Nic grabbed a ladder back chair from the corner of the living room, spun it around and straddled it, resting his arms on the back. His face was bright red either from embarassment or laughing or both.

Lance said, "Now, Preacher, I want you to do as I say, not do as I do." Nic and Lance both burst out laughing again.

"What is going on, guys? You gotta tell me." Their laughing was contagious, and Brian and I were now laughing too.

Tam walked out of her room wearing flannel pajamas that had little red stop signs all over them. I remembered when she bought them at Macy's in Sacramento, but I had never seen her wear them.

"Just for you Pastor Nic," she said as she walked back and forth in front of him like she was on a fashion runway. That got him and Lance to laughing so hard Nic rolled off the chair and onto the floor.

Lance was laughing and snorting. His head bobbed up and down as he said "You have got to be kidding me, Tam. What a perfect ending to a fun-filled, educational, and spiritually uplifting evening with our very own Pastor Nic."

"So what happened?" I said still chuckling. Lance settled in beside me with Brian on the other side. Tam nudged Nic with her bright red polished toes and he got up and took a seat.

"Well. First of all," she started, "where were you two this evening? We missed you at church and you missed a simply marvelous sermon."

"Oh. Tell us about the sermon," I said, hoping to turn the conversation away from my near miss on the speeding ticket.

"Pastor preached another very riveting sermon tonight. He preached on sinning against God. He used the scripture… hold on. Let me think."

Before Tam had time to think Nic said, "*I John 3:4 Whosoever committeth sin transgresseth also the law: for sin is the transgression of the law.*"

"I said to let me think! Gosh!" Tam rolled her eyes and giggled. "Anyway, tonight Nic talked specifically about traffic violations. You know. Like speeding, and running stop signs!" She put a heavy emphasis on "stop signs" and the picture was becoming clearer.

"He said," Tam paused, then continued, " I don't do good Nic impressions, but I'm telling the story so bear with me. He said 'We as Christians must obey the laws of the land, because when we break those laws, we sin against God. I don't want to hear you say 'well everybody else was speeding or nobody stops at that stop sign."

Tam and Lance burst out laughing again and Nic's face turned as red as a ripe tomato.

"On the way over here, Nic made a California stop at the corner just past the church and a policeman was laying in wait." Tam closed her mouth but couldn't hold the laugh in and burst out again.

We were all having a big laugh, and I looked at Brian and asked, "Should we tell them?"

"Tell us what?" Tam, Nic, and Lance all chimed.

"I think you should Nel. It's only right. If the preacher confesses his sin it's only right and good that you do too." he said while trying to keep a straight face.

I made a face at him.

"What's going on? I sense a story!" Nic practically shouted. "Spill it, Nel."

"Well, the reason Brian and I didn't make it to church this evening was…" I paused and you could have heard a pin drop. "I got stopped for speeding!" I buried my head in my hands, pretending to cry.

"Really?" Lance said.

"Yep, really. But the officer extended his grace to me."

Lance said, "Cool." He appeared to be pondering something. He looked at me, then at Nic, then back at me. "Was the cop cute? Be honest!" he instructed as he sensed my hesitation to answer.

"Well, yeah." I nodded. "Yes, he was kinda cute."

Lance's head started bobbing and he said, "It's too bad the pastor didn't get the cute cop!"

The room erupted in laughter again. We were all laughing so hard we were crying.

Tam said, "Uh oh."

"What's wrong Tam?" Nic straightened up and said with a concerned look on his face.

"I think I tinkled myself again."

CHAPTER 25

The following Wednesday afternoon, I pulled up to Lance's house and parked my car. It felt strange not seeing Brian's car parked beside the garage, but I was happy he had found the apartment. He had only been gone two days and I already missed him terribly.

We are going to have to plan weekly dinners or something for all of us to get together. Now that I have friends, God, I don't want to go back to nothing! Not that You aren't enough, but I think You've given me these friends for a reason. If they all keep leaving what am I gonna do?

Amanda was preparing to head back to school the following Saturday and had asked me to help her pack some things from her room. For whatever reason, she seemed to think she needed to pack every last personal item and take it with her to school. I had told her the day before that she should leave a lot of the little stuff at the house but she wouldn't listen. She insisted on packing everything. And so, here I was, standing on her doorstep ready to help yet another of my friends move away from me.

I sighed a deep sigh before ringing the doorbell. *Lord, help me not to break down crying today. That would be great. Thanks!*

Lance opened the door and burst out laughing. "What's up with you? You look like you just dropped your ice cream cone on the sidewalk!" He pulled me into a friendly embrace, still chuckling.

"Stop it! I'm sad!" I whined as I buried my face in his chest.

"I know." He said still chuckling. "But she's not going forever, Nel. "

"Well, no, I know that. But we were all becoming really close and then Brian left and now Amanda! I don't know if I can take any more people leaving."

We stood quietly for a long moment before we heard Amanda call out from the back of the house, "Who is at the door, bro?! Is it Nel?"

Pulling away from Lance I called, "Yeah, it's me! Be right there!"

We stood for another moment in silence before Lance reached out to touch my cheek gently, "Don't worry, Nel. I'm not planning on going anywhere."

Amanda and I spent all afternoon packing her belongings into boxes Lance had brought home from work. We took a short break around four o'clock for sandwiches and iced tea. As we sat in the kitchen, I noticed Amanda was quieter than usual and she appeared to be lost in thought. I wasn't sure if I should ask her what she was thinking or just wait for her to talk.

Um, Abba? I need You now. What am I supposed to do?

I waited. Nothing was coming to me. I sat in silence, chomping my ham sandwich.

Why does lettuce always seem to make so much noise when there's no other noise in the room? Ugh. Chew quieter, Nel! I found myself trying to chew quieter, which only made my lettuce seem even louder. I laid my sandwich down and sipped my tea instead.

Amanda took a deep breath.

"Yes?" I asked a bit too eagerly before she even said anything.

"Huh?"

"Oh. Nothing." I mumbled. "I thought you were gonna say something."

"Oh. Well…" Amanda hesitated. "I was going to, but I'm not sure how to say it."

"Maybe just start talking and it'll come to you."

She took another deep breath before beginning. "How do you feel about Brian?"

Slightly taken aback by the question I asked, "What do you mean?"

"I mean, like… How do you feel about him? Not romantically or anything; I know you guys aren't interested in each other anymore. But how do you think he's doing spiritually and stuff? Is he a good guy?"

"He's like anyone else who's a new Christian, Amanda. He has a lot of growing and learning to do but I think he's doing well. We're all at different stages in our walk with God. I really try not to look at people and 'type' them according to what I think their spiritually is because I can't actually see their heart and know where they are. I can only see the outside of people and that's not the best gauge." I chuckled.

"What's funny?" Amanda asked with a grin on her face.

"I was just thinking of when I met your brother. I totally had the wrong idea about him based on his appearance. He's nothing like I imagined." I could feel a smile spreading across my face.

"You like my brother a lot, don't you."

It wasn't a question. Amanda was stating a fact.

"Yeah." Nodding my head, I admitted aloud for the first time that I liked Lance Dupont, and to his sister nonetheless. "I do, Amanda. I like him *a lot*. Is that weird for you to hear?"

Amanda had a huge smile on her face now. "Not at all! You two are really good together! I'm glad he's found you, Nel. My brother deserves the best, and I think you're it."

"Oh, wow!" Unsure of how to respond, I simply said, "Wow."

Throwing her head back and laughing, Amanda asked, "What's *that* supposed to mean?" Her eyes were sparkling.

"I don't know!" My face was turning bright red. "Lance is a great guy…"

"But?" Amanda urged.

"But… I don't know! I doubt that he likes me *that* much. I think we're just really, really good friends."

"*Whatever!*" Amanda rolled her eyes dramatically. "You are delusional, Nel! My brother is absolutely crazy about you! You're pretty much all he ever talks about. I haven't seen him smile this much or heard him really laugh in a long time. Ever since my grandparents' health has started to decline, he's been down. But then you came along and agreed to one little ol' date and he's a changed man!"

"Really?"

"Yes! Really! You'd better say yes when he proposes, or I'll hunt you down and… and… Well, I'll think up something really cruel and unusual to do to you!"

We both laughed as we headed back to finish packing the rest of her belongings. Outwardly, I was focused on getting things done in time to go to church. Inwardly, I was in turmoil.

God, what's going on? Marriage? I'm not ready for that! Am I? Lance isn't really that serious about me. Is he? He's awesome, Abba, but is he really what You have for me? Please give me patience, Lord — and lots of wisdom!

Saturday morning found us all gathered in Lance's driveway bidding Amanda a tearful farewell. Tam had already given her a hug and a card and was now sitting on the porch steps. Nic had said his goodbye and had wandered over to lean against his car. Amanda grabbed me around my neck and held on tightly.

"Promise to keep in touch, Nel!"

"Of course, I will. I promise."

Both of us were fighting off tears and did not want to let go.

Amanda whispered in my ear, "Be nice to my bro, okay? Take care of him."

Not knowing how to respond, I simply agreed, "I will."

I stepped away and sat down next to Tam in order to give Lance and Amanda time to say goodbye. Tam heard me sniffling and reached her arm around me and then she did something I was not expecting. Tam began to pray.

"Dear God, thanks for bring Nel into my life. She's taught me so much just from watching her life. Thank You for bringing all of us together as friends. I don't understand why You did, but You did... so, thanks. Please help Amanda now as she goes back to school. Keep her safe, please, as she drives and help her get settled in there quickly. Please help all of us to just trust You and not try to control everything on our own. Keep teaching us, God, and help us not to ignore You. Thanks, God. Amen."

Tam squeezed me tightly. It was the first time I had heard Tamara pray; it was so sweet. I could tell she felt slightly awkward doing it, but she was talking to God just like she would to a friend and that's how it ought to be, right? God is our best Friend! I said a quick prayer thanking God for being real in Tam's life and asked Him to continue to teach me.

Amanda was closing her car door when I looked up. We all gathered around Lance and waved as she drove away. We watched her car disappear around the bend in the driveway.

"Well," Lance said as he stuffed his hands in his pockets. "Anyone feel like a road trip to visit my sister at school?"

Everyone laughed half-heartedly. Nic slapped Lance on the back. "She's not gone forever, man."

"I know."

Grinning up at Lance I said, "This speech sounds familiar."

"Oh be quiet." He stuck his tongue out at me.

"Watch it, boy!"

Lance reached out to pull my hair but I dodged away, punching him in the belly as I did.

"Oompf." He doubled over slightly, "You're in for it now!"

I took off running around into the house and Lance came after me.

"Now, now, children!" I heard Nic call after us.

I didn't get the front door closed before Lance was right there, forcing it open. I tried to hide behind the door. It was a bad move. Lance cornered me and I found myself looking up into his face; his finger was pointing in my face, almost touching my nose.

"You, little lady, had better watch it." He said with laughter sparkling in his eyes.

"Or what?" I challenged.

"Or…. Or…. I'll think of something."

I giggled as he grabbed my shoulders and hugged me tightly. "Thanks for being here, Nel. It really means a lot to me."

"Anytime, handsome." *Where did that come from?! What in the world!*

"What did you say?" Lance asked incredulously.

Just then, Nic and Tam came through the door, saving me from having to repeat what had slipped off my tongue. *Thank You, Lord!*

"I need food!" Nic announced as he rubbed his belly. "You got any food in this joint, Lance?"

"Huh?"

"Food. You know, nourishment. The stuff you eat. Do you have any?"

"Oh. Uh, yeah." He shook his head. "Yeah. I think we have stuff for sandwiches in the fridge."

"Well, what doth hinder us from eating, drinking, and being married?" Nic joked.

"Don't you mean 'being merry'?" Tam chuckled.

"Yeah. That too." He laughed as he headed to the kitchen, tossing Lance and me a knowing glance over his shoulder. Tam followed him, chattering about what kind of sandwich sounded good to her.

Lance and I stood in the foyer for a moment before he held out his hand, "Shall we join them?"

"Yes, I think we shall." I placed my hand in his and we headed for the kitchen, both of us wearing Cheshire grins.

We had all eaten our sandwiches, some of us more than others, and were sitting around the kitchen table chatting about life in general. The conversation was casually meandering back and forth between spiritual things and funny stories from college days and childhood. It felt good to be with fellow Christians who were my age - to laugh and pray together. I was overwhelmed again by God's goodness and His love for me. Although two of our friends were now in the Bay area, the four of us could still be friends and feel comfortable with each other; I felt like I could be myself with these friends God had given me. I didn't want anything to change.

Lance's cell phone rang and his brow furrowed as he looked at the caller ID.

"Is everything okay?" I asked.

"Sorry. I need to take this." He said as he stood from the table and headed out the door.

We all looked at each other and shrugged. Our conversation continued although the mood was slightly dampened by our concern for Lance. When he came back in, almost thirty minutes later, I could tell he'd been crying. He stood in the doorway with his hands resting on his waist. He wiped his eyes with one hand and it lingered over his mouth. His head was bowed and he drew several deep breaths.

My heart nearly stopped and my voice rasped as I asked, "What's wrong?"

"I need some time," was his response. "Alone, please."

CHAPTER 26

S omething was terribly wrong. I could hear it in Lance's voice, see it in his eyes. *What should I do Lord? Give me the words to comfort my dear friend. Or should I say nothing? My desire is to do your will Lord and your will is to show love and gentleness.*

I was getting all worked up, which, of course, would benefit no one. I glanced at Nic thinking perhaps he would know what to do. The look on his face was blank; he was as much at a loss as I was. The three of us, me, Nic, and Tam, sat silently together for a couple of minutes.

Tam broke the silence. "Why don't we pray Nic? Um. You know, maybe each of us talk to God and lift Lance up to Him. I'll start and then Nel and you can finish."

"Sounds good," Nic said.

We stood up and took each other's hands. Tam's long and slender smooth fingers were quite a contrast to Nic's semi-rough strong hand. Yet they both had a tender heart and a love for God and for our little pod of friends. That small observation was almost if God was making sure I had learned my lesson about judging based on outward appearances. Our close knit group of six friends had shrunk to four in a matter of a few days, and now, I had this gut feeling that we might be losing another.

Tamara began. "Hey Lord. You know I am new at really talking to you, but I will do the best I can. Father God, You have given me new life with these wonderful friends, and now something serious is happening with Lance. I don't... Uh... We don't know what it is, but I know that You do. Can you please just give him peace in his heart over whatever it is that has stung him? I Love You Lord and I love each of my friends. Thank you for my salvation."

She squeezed my hand to cue me that she was done.

I began, "Abba Father, please help Lance to know and understand that whatever that call was about, that You are still in control. And Father, help me to find ways to bring him joy and comfort in this obvious time of need. In Jesus name."

After a brief pause, Nic continued with our prayer. "God Almighty, all powerful and all knowing. We thank You for our trials and our pains because we know that they strengthen us. We thank you for your watchful eye over us, Your children. Now Jehovah, we ask that You intervene in Lance's life here and now, whatever His need is Lord, we ask that You supply it, because we know that You are the great Physician and You can heal him, if healing is needed, comfort him, if comfort is needed, and give him peace in his life, where peace is needed. In Jesus most holy name. Amen and Amen."

I felt a gentle squeeze of my hands from both Nic and Tam. We continued with our heads bowed sending up our petitions to our God on Lance's behalf.

A hand was gently placed on my shoulder. I opened my eyes and turned my head to see Lance standing there, a deadpan look about his face. His eyes were red and slightly swollen and his cheeks were wet with tears.

I squeezed Tam's hand and then Nic's and they released my hands. I turned and faced Lance and he rested his chin on the top of my head as we embraced. I could see Nic glance at Tam and then nod and I closed my eyes as I felt Tam and Nic press up against us, arms extending all around Lance, in a demonstration of God's command to love one another. Lance tried to maintain his composure, but our show of affection towards him was more than he could bear, and he broke down and cried.

When Lance's tears began to subside, we sat down. Tam and I sat on each side and gently rubbed Lance's back and shoulders. Nic pulled up a chair in front of Lance. Any other time, Nic would have spun the chair around, straddled it, and leaned his arms on the back. A different side of Nic was needed now. He sat facing Lance, their knees almost touching. He leaned forward and took Lance's right hand and held it with both his hands and said, "Brother. Is there anything I can do for you *right* now?"

Lance lightly shook his head.

"Well my friend and brother in Christ, if you need anything, for me to pray with you, a shoulder to cry on, an ear to listen to you, or just someone to be present with you, please call on me."

Lance slowly stood up; Nic stood up to meet him. They were toe to toe, and Lance wrapped his arms around him and said, "Thank you Pastor."

Tam and I got up and began to walk towards the front door. Nic turned to follow.

Lance looked at me and said, "Nelia. Will you stay a while longer?"

"Sure I will," I said as I turned and walked back toward him and reached for his hand as he waved bye to Nic and Tam.

"I got some terrible news," Lance began. "My grandfather Miles, my dad's dad had a massive stroke at the farm in Newcastle, Delaware. My grandma found him and he was rushed to St. Francis in Wilmington where they have him on life support."

"What are you going to do?" I asked.

"My Uncle Johnny who lives in Manhattan has a ticket waiting at Sacramento International Airport for me to get on the a flight to Wilmington tonight."

"What time does your flight leave and do you need a ride?"

"Leaving at… Wait a second."

Lance fumbled around in his pocket and pulled out a piece of paper that looked like it had kid scribbling on it.

"Here it is. Let's see. US Airways Flight 378. Hmmm. Can't make this out. Oh. There it is. 10:25. It leaves at 10:25."

I looked at my watch. "Lance. It's 6:15 now. You better pack some things. What can I do?"

"Can you take me to the airport?"

"Absolutely! Let me text Tam and see if she can bring my car over and we can drop her back at the apartment on the way out of town."

"No Nel. That's not necessary. Just take my car."

"What? No way. I can't drive your car! Are you kidding me?"

"Yes."

"I knew it. Yes you were kidding me."

"No Nel. I wasn't kidding you. Yes. You can drive my car."

"You mean you would trust me with it?"

"Nel. Nel. You should know that if a man can trust a woman with his heart, he can trust her with his car."

I felt my face flush. I wanted to look into Lance's eyes, but fought the urge. For some odd reason, I felt vulnerable.

He pulled me to him and said, "I love you."

Lance went to pack his things while I went to the kitchen and made some coffee. I sat down and thought about what Lance had said.

I love you can mean many different things. I say I love you to my sister, to my dad and mom. I say I love you to my roommate Tam, even to Figaro, my cat. So what exactly did Lance mean when he said 'I love you'?

I took Lance a cup of coffee. He was fitfully throwing things into a duffel bag, and he didn't hear me coming. I heard him mumbling something that resembled him having an argument with God.

He was saying, "I know Lord, but why now? Yeah I do get it. I know it's not about me. I know you are preparing me for bigger and better things, but why did this have to happen right now when I was feeling so close to Nel. You told me you would give me a *Proverbs 31* woman, and now after all summer of us getting close, you throw this little trial at me."

I knocked lightly on the door and said, "Everything okay?

I handed him the piping hot coffee that he smelled when I entered the room. "Yeah. I am about ready. How did you know this was just what I needed?"

"Woman's intuition?" I said in the form of a question. "And I have two to-go cups in the kitchen so we don't spill anything in that gorgeous car of yours."

"Oh and she thinks ahead. I like that!" He chuckled slightly and I could sense that my presence had somewhat eased his mind.

We were on the road by seven. Lance had put the top down and the wind on my face felt good. We sat in silence for the first ten minutes of the ride. I couldn't stand it any longer. A question was burning in my mind.

"Lance?"

"Yes?"

"Do you know when you will be back?"

"Well, I can't say for sure. Maybe a week. Maybe two."

"But you *are* coming back right?"

"Of course I am. But right now there are a lot of things up in the air. If grandpa dies, I may have to go back for a long while to take care of my grandma. She depends on grandpa. I don't know what she will do when he's gone."

"Are they believers? I mean are they saved?"

"Oh yeah. And my grandma will be fine knowing that grandpa is in a better place. I just think she will hope to meet my grandpa in heaven sooner than later. After all, she would then be with her son…" Lance choked up and tears began to stream his cheeks. "…my daddy too. And she would finally know…" He paused and wiped the tears from his face. "…why it had to be daddy and momma that had to die that day."

I was visibly moved and grasped Lance's hand and held it tightly.

"Lance. You amaze me. You have such a gentleness about you and such a love for God. Your faith is way stronger than mine."

"Nel," he said as he reached over and wiped a trailing tear from my cheek, "you are the amazing one, the strong force of influence in all those that are around you. Look at Tam and Brian how their lives have changed dramatically. Even Nic's disposition has been altered by the force field that comes from you."

"Give God the glory Lance, not me."

"Oh I do. And I thank him every hour for using use as a reflection of the character he wants to see in us."

We drove the rest of the way silently. I wondered what Lance was thinking and I'm sure he wondered about what thoughts passed through my mind.

Lance pulled up to the terminal and got out. He ran around and opened my door and then reached in the back seat and grabbed his bag. I put my arms around his waist and layed my head against his chest. It gave me a peace to feel his heart beating.

His kissed me on the forehead. I pulled his face down to mine and kissed him lightly on the lips, then said, "Don't forget about me."

"Don't worry Nelia. I could never forget about you," he said as he turned and rushed into the terminal.

Sunday morning came early. I had texted Tam on the way to the airport to let her know what was going on. When I got back from the airport she was up and we had had a late night chat about guys and things and more importantly about how God had been working in all of our lives.

When I woke up, I felt sad and lonely. Tam knocked on my door and was ready for church.

"Get up Nel," she said through the door. "We don't want to be late."

"I don't feel like going."

"Nelia Lynn Chambers!" She said as she flung open my door. "Don't you know that that's the best time *to* go to church – when you don't feel like going," she said with a lady-like southern drawl.

Oh my soul. That is exactly the thing I used to say to her, I thought. *Payback time.*

"You are absolutely right. I'll be ready in twenty minutes," I said.

Nic greeted us as we entered the church building. We were five minutes early. We made our way down to the middle of the sanctuary and sat on the left. It felt so different without Brian and Amanda and now without Lance. I wanted to get up and leave.

The songleader began with a contemporary song *Heart of Worship*. I closed my eyes, and the words of the song became my prayer.

> *When the music fades*
> *All is stripped away*
> *And I simply come*
> *Longing just to bring*
> *Something that's of worth*
> *That will bless Your heart*
>
> *I'll bring You more than a song*
> *For a song in itself*
> *Is not what You have required*
> *You search much deeper within*
> *Through the way things appear*
> *You're looking into my heart*
>
> *I'm coming back to the heart of worship*
> *And it's all about You,*
> *It's all about You, Jesus*
> *I'm sorry, Lord, for the thing I've made it*
> *When it's all about You,*
> *It's all about You, Jesus*

I felt the corners of my mouth begin to turn up and I looked up and mouthed those last words again. "It's all about You Jesus."

Nic's preaching had never been dull, and as he made his way to the pulpit, I sensed that today his sermon was going to be even more uplifting. All summer long, he had challenged the congregants to move out of their comfort zones and serve, to question their attitudes towards God and each other, and to extend forgiveness without reservation.

"I have witnessed a lot of damaged souls in our very own midst the summer," he began. "A lot of hurt, a lot of hurt feelings, and a whole lot of brokenness. But the Lord has shared something with me this morning. He has laid on my heart today, a lesson, one that we have all heard as toddlers, one that each and every one of us can relate to. How many of you know the story of Humpty Dumpty?"

There was chattering throughout the room and giggles from the little children.

"Then you know about how Humpty Dumpty sat on a wall and how he had a great fall. And I would venture to say that each of you out there have experienced disappointments, bad experiences, broken lives. I am certain that many of you are experiencing brokenness in your life or your relationship or your job today."

Nic moved to the center aisle and began pacing up and down.

"You know how the story of Humpty Dumpty ends." He paused before continuing. "All the King's horses and all the King's men, couldn't put Humpty Dumpty back together again."

He made his way back to the pulpit, took a deep breath and said, "But we serve a King that is in the business of fixing broken lives! He repairs broken hearts…"

I heard the sanctuary door open, and Nic's expression turned to one of amazement. I turned to look over my shoulder. The ushers were standing holding the large doors to the sanctuary open. I looked in disbelief as Brian entered the sanctuary with his arm over his dad's shoulder.

I could hardly recognize Mr. Gentry; the effects of alcohol and a life based on deceit had aged and weathered the once stylish and handsome father.

Brian saw me and I scooted over. He sat down beside me and turned and we hugged. His cheeks were wet with tears and he said, "Hi Nel."

Mr. Gentry didn't stop and sit next to Brian. He continued walking slowly but deliberately until he reached the altar where he dropped to his knees and pressed his forehead down on the altar.

Nic continued his preaching.

"Our King can take all your pieces, no matter how broken you are, and if you yield to Him, He can put you back together better than new. He fixes broken relationships. He heals broken hearts. If you are broken, in pain, have an unforgiving heart, the King of Kings, the great Physician can heal you today. Right here and right now."

Brian was unaware that his father had gone to the altar. His eyes were closed as he held me tight.

I whispered to him, "Brian. Your dad's at the altar praying."

Brian got up immediately and went to the altar, knelt by his dad and put his arm over his dad's shoulder.

I felt the Spirit tugging at me and I got up and headed to the altar; Tamara was right behind me. Others, Sandi and Jim, the lady with the big blue hat came down as we gathered around Mr. Gentry each praying for guidance, wisdom, healing, and love.

Nic continued preaching and read from *Jeremiah 18*.

"1 The word which came to Jeremiah from the LORD, saying, 2 Arise, and go down to the potter's house, and there I will cause thee to hear my words. 3 Then I went down to the potter's house, and, behold, he wrought a work on the wheels. 4 And the vessel that he made of clay was marred in the hand of the potter: so he made it again another vessel, as seemed good to the potter to make it. 5 Then the word of the LORD came to me, saying, 6 O house of Israel, cannot I do with you as this potter? saith the LORD. Behold, as the clay is in the potter's hand, so are ye in mine hand, O house of Israel. The Lord is saying that any flaws, any brokenness, any impurities that are in your life can be fixed. Just let Him have his way with you."

I was amazed at what spiritual healings took place that morning. And they continued as the song leader got up and sang *Softly and Tenderly Jesus is Calling*.

That evening Brian called me.

"Why didn't you tell me you had spoken to your dad? That he was coming out here," I asked.

"It was something I had to do on my own. Well. Not without God," he said.

"I knew what you meant. So what's going on?"

"I am taking dad to Stanford tomorrow morning. He is going into a new rehab program they have there. It was all his idea after I called him and told him, I wanted us to start over again. He said he wanted to break all ties with his old friends and if I would help him, he would stay straight. Last night was the first time since I was a little boy that dad and I prayed together."

"Oh. I am so happy for you Brian," I said fighting back tears.

"It's going to be a long and a hard road Nel. Please pray for me and my dad."

"You know I will."

"Oh, and Nel? Pray that Amanda and Lance will find a way to forgive him. By the way, where was Lance this morning?"

I explained to Brian what Lance was going through. My call waiting beeped and I looked at the caller ID.

"I gotta go, that's Lance."

CHAPTER 27

H ey Lance. How are you?" I said.

"Not good. My connecting flight was delayed in Charlotte, and I made it to the hospital too late."

"Your grandfather passed away?"

"Yeah Nel. I'm sure gonna miss him. He was a real good man, and now..." He paused momentarily.

"What Lance? You are coming home aren't you?" I felt selfish saying that.

"As soon as the funeral is over Thursday, I am catching a plane back to Sacramento. I have a lot I need to talk to you about before I come back."

"What do you mean 'come back?'"

"I mean, I have to come back to take care of my grandmother. Can't we talk about it when you pick me up Thursday?"

"Yes," I said sounding distraught. "Do you have your flight information yet?"

"No. I'll text it to you though when I have my ticket."

"Okay."

"I need to get some sleep Nel. I am wiped out."

"Alright," I said as if I just lost my best friend.

"Oh and Nel?" Lance said.

"Yes Lance, " I conjured up some cheer.

"I haven't forgot about you. I'll talk to you tomorrow."

That put a smile on my face.

"Okay, good night."

The next four days passed by like molasses flowed on a cold winter Wisconsin morning. I was going crazy waiting for Lance to come home, and I was snappy with everyone. Even Figaro. No man had ever had that effect on me before.

Why do I feel the way I do with Lance gone Lord?

Thursday morning before work, I decided to give Rachel a call.

The phone rang four rings and I started to hang up.

"Hello," Rachel answered just before I hung up.

"Hey sis."

"Uh. Oh. What's wrong? No. Let me guess. Sounds like a woman in love who is missing her man. Am I warm?"

"Shut up sis," I said jokingly. "How did you know?"

"Oh that's easy Nel. I'm a woman in love and my man is away on a business trip. Where's Lance?"

I explained to Rachel all that had happened with Lance, and all she could say was "Praise God."

"I'm not quite sure I get you Rachel. How can you be that way? Don't you feel sorry at all for Lance?" I said with a bit of indignation.

"Of course I do Nel. I am not being cold or anything. The Bible teaches us to take joy in our trials and afflictions. Don't you see the great work He is doing in your life and Lance's and Tam's?"

I remembered Sunday morning seeing Brian with his dad and added, "And Brian's." Then I went on to explain what had happened with Brian extending forgiveness to his dad. She shouted over the phone, "Praise God!"

The conversation with Rachel had eased my tension so I was more tolerable at work that day.

Lance texted me at two oclock. He was at the airport getting ready to board the plane.. He was arriving at 10:40pm on U.S. Airways flight 377. He ended his text with *cant wait 2 c u btw hows my car?* ☺ That made me smile.

I watched as the second hand advanced around the clock.

Five o'clock is taking forever!

I got up and rearranged all the travel brochures in the rack to pass the time. When five oclock finally rolled around, I said bye to Jim and Sandi and headed home for a shower and to change.

When I emerged from my room, I felt fresh and invigorated. I was wearing white capris and a peach sleeveless blouse. I had my hair tied back in a ponytail and I was wearing my *Daisy Fuentes* sandals. I was checking my toenail polish as I walked into the living room and was greeted by Nic and Tam.

"Woo. Sexy." Tam said.

"Who's the lucky man?" Nic asked. "Wait. Let me guess."

He looked at Tam, smiled, and then looked back at me. "I bet it's Lancie boy," he said.

"Is that your final answer?" Tam asked into an imaginary microphone.

"Cute guys. Real cute," I said with a smile.

"No. That's what Lance will be saying tonight when he picks you up chica. Cute. Real cute. Extremely cute!" Tam said as she laughed.

"Cut it out guys."

"Want us to go with you?" Nic asked. "You know, Nel. As your pastor, I would probably be about the best chaperone you could find."

"I can attest to that," Tam chimed in.

"Oh do tell," I said with a chuckle.

"Yes," Nic said. "Do tell!"

U.S. Airways flight 377 was on time, and I was waiting at the curb when Lance came out of the terminal. I leaped into his arms and gave him a big kiss.

"I really missed you Lance."

"Really? Not as much as I missed you though."

Lance threw his bag into the back seat and we got in the car. As he pulled away from the curb, he took my hand in his and said, "There's no good time or easy way to tell you this."

My heart sunk.

"I have to go back to Delaware next week. Uncle Johnny is staying with grandma right now, but he has to go back to Manhattan to his family and work and there's no one else to stay with my grandmother."

I sat there staring straight ahead at the road. I wanted to cry, and I wanted to scream. I didn't want Lance to leave and be gone for a long time.

I continued looking straight ahead and asked dryly, "For how long?"

"A couple of months. Six months at most."

I spun in my seat towards Lance and said, "Six months? What am I supposed to do?"

He said in a calm, matter of fact voice, "Wait for me."

"Wait for you? Are you kidding me? I am just…" I stopped myself. "I'm so sorry Lance. It's just that I have been thinking a lot about you, about us, since you have been gone."

"Us? Wow. It must be true what they say. Absence *does* makes the heart grow fonder. I'm glad to hear you say *us* like we are a couple."

"Yeah. But now your going to be gone."

"It's not like I'm gonna be gone forever," Lance said with a chuckle.

I couldn't resist; I stuck my tongue out at him.

Lance said he needed to go back to Delaware in a week. He told me that if I was afraid he wouldn't come back, he would leave his red Camaro in my care. That could be my insurance.

I wanted to spend every waking moment with Lance until he had to leave again. While I was at work Friday, he took care of all his affairs here in Jackson, tying up loose ends. He came over to the apartment after I got home from work and we watched a movie together. I had made it known to Tam that I needed time alone with Lance. She understood.

We went to Stanford Saturday morning to visit with Amanda and take her a few of the odds and ends she had forgot to pack. Lance updated her on what was happening back east, and we left early afternoon to go back to Jackson. Lance said he wanted to cook dinner for me that evening and had a surprise for me, "or two" as he put it.

On the ride home, I closed my eyes and wondered when and how God would reveal to me if Lance was the one that God had specifically designed for me.

"Lance?"

"Yes?"

"What do you think this means for us? You know. You having to go back east for a while."

"I don't know Nel. What I do know though is that if we are living God's will, and not our own, He will reveal our path and light the way."

Boy. How do I respond to that?

I sat silently pondering Lance's statement. I felt the corners of my mouth turn up in a smile.

"Yeah. I guess you're right Lance."

"You guess I'm right," he retorted. "You know I'm right."

He squeezed my hand.

I had Lance drop me off at my apartment to shower and change for what he announced was the "big event of the evening."

He said, "I'll be back to pick you up at eight, and don't make me wait."

I turned as I was walking away from the car and asked, "What shall I wear? Is it a black tie event?"

"How about that bright blue sundress? You look stunning in it?"

"Why thank you. The blue sundress it will be."

"Oh and Nelia. Will you leave your hair down?"

"Of course I will. Whatever you wish."

I was nervous with excitement and anticipation when Lance arrived. He wore knee length khaki cargo shorts and a blue button down collared shirt. His hair was tied back in a ponytail and although his physical appearance had changed very little since that first time I saw him in Starbucks, he was a different man. God had opened my eyes to the true Lance, not the Lance that I had passed judgment on. *Thank you Father for showing me this gentle Christian man.*

When we arrived at Lance's place, I could see on the southern side of the porch he had set a table for two with candles, his mother's Havilland china, and cloth napkins. *Lord, forgive me for having been so quick to judge this man.*

Lance had prepared a recipe of fresh seafood he had bought while back east; he had it air-freighted packed in dry ice (He told me later.) Maryland blue crab crabcakes and Chincoteague oysters, as well as clams and scallops which he had added to his grandma Dupont's *Seafood Alfredo* recipe. He had also prepared his scrumptious asparagus spears and had sliced tomatoes from his small garden behind the house.

We dined quietly together as we watched the full golden harvest moon rise in the southeastern sky. I finally broke the silence.

"If this dinner is one surprise and the full moon as a backdrop is the other, you totally outdid yourself Lance Dupont."

"Well thank you. But those aren't the surprises."

"Okay then. Give it up. The suspense is killing me," I said as I slapped the table.

"Patience my dear Nel. Patience my friend," He stacked his plate on top of mine and then moved the plates to the corner of the table. Reaching under the table, he produced a large coffee table type book and placed it in front of me. The cover was engraved with the title *The Story of Penny a Page,* by Nelia Lynn Chambers. Underneath was the inscription, Foreword by Lance Dupont, and there was a picture of the front of his house.

"What is this?" I asked. My stomach was doing flips, not because of the food, but because of what I thought Lance was trying to tell me.

"Open it up."

I opened it and the first page was titled *Chapter 1- Lease Agreement.*

"That's very sweet of you Lance but I can't afford to lease this place while you're gone, and besides, where would you stay when you get back?

"Read it. Read the terms. Or do you want me to tell you what the terms are?"

I took a sip of ice water. "It's just a dream Lance."

"Yes, Nel. But I can help you make the dream a reality."

"No. I can't Lance." *Or can I? Is this Your way of using me in the community? Talk to me Lord.*

"Listen Nel. God has blessed me immensely. Things have been taken from me, granted. My parents, the biggest thing, but then years later God placed you in my path, and I believe that this is his plan for you and his plan for me to help. To answer your second question first, this house is two stories with a basement. The upstairs has an outside entrance in the back. You've been upstairs and down the stairs out back. I can live upstairs, the bookstore and coffee shop can be downstairs and you can use the basement to store your inventory and supplies. The lease is for only five years."

"But I can't even afford five days rent."

"Oh yes you can. The monthly rent is zero dollars."

"I can't Lance."

"Oh yes you can Nel. If it will make you feel better, consider me your silent partner."

"But I can't run the place by myself and I don't have money to pay anyone. Plus I don't have money to buy books. A bookstore needs books."

"Not a problem Nel. Michelle and Frank at Starbucks have agreed to work for you and I will cover their salary for a year. Frank is an excellent barista and Michelle can work the coffee area and help you with the bookstore end."

"Is Michelle the one with all the tattoos and piercings?" I asked

"No. She's the giggling blonde."

"Oh good."

Lance looked irritated. "Is there something wrong with Ariana?"

"Who's Ariana?

"Tattoos, piercings."

"Well. She looks kind of scary," I said.

"Nelia! You should be ashamed of yourself. She's actually a very nice girl and has been asking me about church and talking about the Lord."

Oops. Sorry Lord. I still need work in that area.

"Sorry Lance. And thank you for your offer. But I still need a several thousand dollars for renovation and inventory. I can't let you do that much for me."

"Don't worry. That base is covered too. I called Brian, and he said he was sure he could arrange for a small business loan to get you off the ground.

Oh, and Tam said she will help set up the renovation and help you with the interior design."

"You're kidding? Brian and Tam know about this?"

"Yes Nel. They are your friends. They want to help you realize your dream."

"Lance." I looked him square in the eyes and held his fingertips with mine. "This is beyond my wildest dreams. I don't know if I can accept this."

"Nel. This is your dream. Accept my invitation to make it a reality."

I stood up and he stood up and stepped to the side to meet me. I wrapped my arms around his waist and looked up at him. "Okay Lance. I'll accept, and then I kissed him. I felt overwhelmed with emotion. As we pulled apart and sat down, Lance said, "Ready for surprise number two?"

Surprise number one was still soaking in. It would be weeks before it I would realize that *Penny a Page* was no longer a dream; it was a reality. God had placed Lance in my life knowing our capacities as human beings to benefit each other for the furtherance of His Kingdom.

Did I dare guess what Lance had in store next?

"I'm as ready as I'm gonna be. After all, what could top surprise number one?" I said.

Lance stood up and moved his chair to the side of the table and angled it toward mine. He reached under the table again, this time producing a little box with a blue ribbon around it tied in a bow. A shiny new penny was glued to the center of the bow.

I felt my face flush and I thought I might faint. I took another sip of water and looked at Lance nervously.

He said, "Open it."

My hands were visibly shaking as I pulled the ribbon off and removed the lid from the white box. Inside was a smaller box, antique looking and ornate.

I looked at Lance. He had a slight smile.

"Go ahead Nel. Open it," he coaxed me.

Slowly I lifted the lid. My mouth fell open. The light of the moon illuminated a beautiful clear, two carat marquis diamond set in white gold.

"It's… it's beautiful.," I said with a whisper.

"It was my mom's," Lance said as he dropped to one knee. "Will you marry me Nelia Lynn Chambers?"

"I need a minute Lance. I need to go to the bathroom."

I grabbed my purse, then ran in the house and into the bathroom. I lifted the toilet seat and sat down. I texted Tam. *He askd me 2 marry him.* I sat there waiting for a response. A minute passed. No response.

I called Rachel. On the second ring I heard, "Hello?" It was after midnight, but I knew Rachel would want to know.

"Rachel. Lance asked me to marry him," I said in an excited whisper.

That woke her up!

"That's great. Praise the Lord. When's the date?"

"I haven't said yes yet."

"Hang up and go say yes and then call me back," she said, and then she disconnected.

I heard Lance outside the door. "Is everything okay?"

"Yep, everything is fine. I'll be right out."

My phone vibrated, I jumped, and the phone slipped from my hand right into the toilet. "Oh no!" I said.

Lance was still outside the door.

"Are you sure your okay? I'm coming in Nel."

The door flung open and Lance stood there with his eyes closed.

"Are you decent?"

"Yes Lance, you can open your eyes."

I held my arms open, an invitation for him to hold me. We embraced for a long moment before I looked up at him and said, "Yes I'll marry you Lance Dupont."

He picked me up and spun me around. When he set me down he looked at me and said, "Your phone is in the toilet."

"I know."

He looked at me and grinned from ear to ear

"Oh Nel. What am I going to do with you?"

"You're going to take me to T-Mobile first thing Monday morning so I can get a new cell phone. I've got a wedding to plan."

It was the perfect evening to a summer that was, in God's eyes, the perfect plan for molding us and making us, me, Lance, Tamara, Nic, Amanda, and Brian, men and women in his likeness.

Lance said the evening had turned out just the way he had hoped. I had not realized until that night why Lance pointed out the moon whenever he could. That evening, he shared with me how his dad had taken him out often to look at the moon. He said it was a sweet reminder that God was in control. His dad had explained to him that the tides were controlled by the moon and that the rhythms of living things relied on the moon's phases. Lance told me that if I would grant him one wish for the wedding, it would be that we pick a date when we could get married by the light of the full moon.

Watch for the sequel to Single Shot

Double Shot

To be released in December 2011

ISBN-13: 978-0615515496

ISBN-10: 0615515495

The following is a sneak preview of *Double Shot*.

Double Shot

CHAPTER 1

Six months had passed since Lance boarded the plane that carried him away from me. At the time, I was upset and did not understand why God would bring us together only to separate us again; it seemed too cruel. But now I understood. So much had changed in my life since that day in August and I found myself thanking God at every turn for manifesting His will in my life.

Penny A Page was quickly becoming the new local hangout. The renovations hadn't taken long at all since we simply pulled all the furniture away from the walls on the lower level and made all the walls built-in bookshelves. I had sold some of the larger furniture pieces and replaced them with overstuffed chairs and loveseats nestled amongst the books. End tables carrying vintage lamps were scattered around the rooms to make readers feel cozy and at home while also providing ample light for reading any number of the used books which had found their way onto my shelves.

The coffee bar had been a great success as well. Michelle was a miracle worker when it came to anything coffee; she knew her way around an upside-down caramel macchiato even better than Lance, but don't tell him I said that. Michelle had a way about her that made everyone feel right at home as soon as they stepped foot in *Penny A Page*. She also had a deep love and appreciation for a good book, which made her a great asset to have around when I was hitting all the estate sales, buying up all the old books for the shop. She had found a good many beautifully bound classics that now adorned our shelves. Michelle was truly a God-send.

Frank had been a huge help as well, making sure all the shelves were in order and able to hold the heavy books. He also helped with the upkeep of the house since I was the only one living there and had no idea how to use a hammer, let alone a cordless drill.

Lance made sure both Frank and Michelle were paid every week and that I had enough money to cover all the needed supplies for the coffee bar and to keep the bookshelves full. On top of everything he'd already done to show his love, Lance made sure a beautiful bouquet of Gerbera Daisies, my favorite flower, was delivered to the shop every Monday morning. He also sent long, hand-written letters at least once a week which I kept in an ornate hatbox I had found at one of the estate sales.

Lance Dupont was nothing I had expected, but he was everything I needed.

Just three days before Valentine's Day, Amanda called.

"Hey, Nel!"

"Hey, you! How's it going? Haven't heard from you in a while."

"Yeah. I'm really sorry about that. Things have been crazy around here, but in a good way."

"Well, that's good." I breathed a prayer of thanks. God had been doing some serious work in Amanda's life and it was apparent by her happy disposition. "So what's up, chica?"

"Not a whole lot. I'm actually ahead on my papers and things and so I thought I might come home for a few days. Would that be okay?"

"Okay?!" I nearly shouted. "I can't wait to see you! When are you coming? Frank actually installed one of those chair lift things just last week! Oh, I can't wait to see you."

Amanda giggled into the receiver. "I'm excited to see you too, Nel. It's been way too long."

"Yeah, it has. You're going to love the shop. It looks completely different now with all the shelves and the coffee bar. Oh! And for Valentine's Day we have a sale going on; buy two books, get two coffees free. Hopefully, it'll encourage couples to relax together and just enjoy being in each other's company without the guy being stuck watching a girl movie or the girl being stuck watching football," I said laughing. "What do you think?"

"I love it! Everyone can choose a book they actually like and still be together. It's perfect, Nel!" I heard Amanda sigh on her end. "If only I had a special someone to sit beside and essentially ignore."

I burst into laughter. "I never thought of it *that* way, but I guess that is what we're encouraging."

"Yeah. But it's good! Everyone needs to get lost in their own little world every once in a while; it helps everything else seem better somehow. You can find love between the pages of a book even when you can't in real life."

"Amanda – "

"Not like, God's love, of course, but like… human companionship." She explained.

"I see."

There was silence on the line for several moments. I wasn't sure how to respond. Amanda had gone from happy-go-lucky to slightly depressing in a matter of moments.

What should I do, Lord? Should I say something now or just wait till she's here? Sometimes face-to-face is better, right? What would Lance do? Wait! Dumb question. Sorry, Lord. What would YOU do?

I decided to wait till Amanda was home to figure out what was going on with her.

Putting a smile on my face to mask my worry, I asked, "So when do you think you'll head this way?"

"Maybe this afternoon? I figure if I head that way around one o'clock I'll be there long before dark and I'll miss the majority of the traffic."

"Sounds good to me. I'll make sure your new room is ready for you."

After Amanda and I hung up, I said another prayer for wisdom and headed upstairs to make sure her room was in order; I decided to use the new chair lift, just because I could.

Hmm Works great! Boy, that was kinda fun too. Nel, stop it. You cannot ride that thing all the time or you'll be 500 pounds by the time Lance comes home; you need the exercise so just climb the dang stairs!

I glanced in the floor-length mirror hanging on the back of Amanda's door and was not pleased to see my chubby figure staring back at me. Something had to be done about this before Lance came home – whenever that happened to be.

Amanda arrived slightly earlier than I expected but I was ready. We sat on the porch sipping fresh homemade lemonade and eating cucumber sandwiches. A steady stream of customers entered the shop and several stopped to greet Amanda and me before heading inside in search of a treasure.

One customer, however, shared the porch with us. Every time I saw Mrs. Babstock she made me laugh. Mrs. Babstock was well into her eighties and insisted on everyone calling her Babbie. No one ever saw Babbie without that big straw hat with the red flower right in the front. I would never forget how she welcomed me that first Sunday at Straight Paths when I snuck into church and slipped in beside her. She looked harmless and sweet, but Babbie was sharp as whip and not afraid to say whatever God told her to say. She had quickly become one of my most trusted counselors since Lance went away.

I stood and went inside to pour Amanda and I fresh glasses of lemonade and, when I returned, I found Babbie standing in front of Amanda with her hands clasped tightly around one of Amanda's and she was earnestly praying. Tears flowed down Amanda's face. Leaving the two alone, I retreated into the house and said a prayer of my own.

Abba, I don't know what's going on here, but You do. Please use Babbie in a way that only You can do. Touch Amanda in the short time she's here and help her feel complete in You, God — the way You've made me feel. I love you, God. Amen.

Later on that evening, I could see a great storm brewing Northwest of us and heading our direction. We hadn't had a storm like this in several months. The dark clouds were forming a massive bank on the horizon and I could feel the thunder rattling my bones. I went through the old house, checking windows and doors to make sure we were secured for the night. Frank had offered to stay with us but I refused and told him to go home to be with his wife. I was sure Amanda and I would be fine on our own, despite the storm.

By the time nine o'clock came, hailstones were beating against all the windows and lightning flashes were mere seconds apart. The entire house was shaken to the core and Amanda and I were shaken right along with it. I hadn't experienced a storm like this one since I was a small child back in Wisconsin. That storm had brought with it softball sized hailstones and several barns were burnt to the ground from being struck by lightning.

I found myself crawling into Amanda's bed and holding her as we both tried to remain calm. I had tried to reach Frank on both the landline and on my cell but all the lines and towers must have been down as none of my calls would connect. Amanda and I lay cuddled under her covers, praying and singing, when suddenly we heard a loud crash.

"What was that?" Amanda sounded absolutely terrified. I had to be strong.

"Um… It sounded like maybe a hailstone hit one of the windows." I tried to sound cool, calm, and collected but I could tell I was failing miserably.

"Don't go down there, Nel! Please!" Sensing the fear in her voice, I tried calming her nerves.

"I'm just going to move the books out of the way of that broken window. I don't want any of them ruined from the rain." I assured her. "I'll be right back. I promise."

Feeling my way along the wall, for by now the power lines were down as well, I slowly made my way down the stairs and into the kitchen where I knew I had stored a flashlight in the pantry. I could hear the rain beating against the house and through a broken window somewhere as I found my way to the pantry. The wind whipped around the house creating an eerie howling sound. Occasionally, I could hear a loud pop as a hailstone would hit the house and bounce off.

Suddenly, I heard another noise. This noise stopped me dead in my tracks. I tried breathing as shallow as possible, straining to make sure I was hearing correctly. Only the storm howled around me and then, suddenly, there it was again! Footsteps. It sounded as though someone were crunching broken glass beneath their feet as they took slow, tentative steps.

Oh, God, what am I going to do?

I felt myself begin panicking.

Why on earth did I send Frank home? What was I thinking?!

I mentally shook myself. *Nel, this is no time to zone out! Focus!*

There it was again. Slow, deliberate footsteps. I had to find the flashlight. Making my way closer to the pantry, I tried to make as little noise as possible. My hand hit something hard and I heard the broom crash to the floor. My breath caught in my throat and my heart stopped beating. I listened. Silence. Then, suddenly, I heard the footsteps approaching quickly from the direction of the front room. I didn't have much time. I made a dash in the direction of the pantry. I was too slow. I felt two hands grab my shoulders and made a split second decision; my only course of action was to fight for my life.

About the Authors

Aspiring author, Laura Wagenschutz, was raised in Northern Wisconsin where the long, snowy winters encouraged hours of reading and multiple steamy cups of joe to get her through the chilly evenings. But, before she was old enough to drink coffee or read a great American classic, Laura's dad actually paid her one penny per page for every book she read. Her love of literature quickly developed as her vivid imagination was encouraged by both her parents and her high school principal, Benjamin Jossund. Her appreciation of the written word has developed into a consuming passion that is driven by multiple quad, upside-down caramel macchiatos every day.

Laura currently resides in Southern California where she attends Bible College with a major in Secondary Education, English.

Award-winning author W. Mark Dendy inherited his father's love and ability for telling a good story. Dendy was born and raised in the Mississippi delta where storytelling abounds like fish frys and coon hunts. His narratives bring both tears and laughter to the reader, and his descriptive telling ability transports the reader into the story. His love for God is evident in his writing where he brings scenes to life and fills them with colorful characters.

His creativity is fueled by quad, grande, extra hot, non-fat, no whip, white mochas. When he's not writing, he spends time with his wife, two sons and daughter, and spoils his three Chihuahuas and two cats.

Dendy, a former college adjunct biology professor, is a part-time Missionary Baptist minister where he lives in Elk Grove, California. His memoir, *The Cascade Effect,* (ISBN- 1451547056) won the Best Biography/Autobiography Award at the 2010 Paris Book Festival.